Mama!

Enjoy my story

Love & best wishes

Patricia

(Aust - Brennan

HOLD MY HAND

(Rose's Memories)

Patricia Aust-Brennan

ISBN 0-7414-5164-6

Published by:

INFINITY
PUBLISHING.COM

1094 New DeHaven Street, Suite 100
West Conshohocken, PA 19428-2713
Info@buybooksontheweb.com
www.buybooksontheweb.com
Toll-free (877) BUY BOOK
Local Phone (610) 941-9999
Fax (610) 941-9959

Printed in the United States of America

Printed on Recycled Paper

Published January 2009

Dedication

I dedicate this book to Duncan, Louise, Benjamin, Thomas, and Tess.

You are my bloodline.

Acknowledgments

Special thanks to Duncan, Sylvaine, Louise, Laurence, Jim, Yolande, and all who encouraged me to write this story.

A SENTIMENTAL JOURNEY

The limo driver rang the doorbell; the clock on the kitchen wall was just striking 10 a.m. I knew him very well as I had used this service several times over the past few years. I opened the door and said, "Good morning, Frankie. My bags are here, just the two blue ones." He smiled as he shook his head and said, "I never thought you would actually go through with this. I thought you were settled here, and you seemed very happy." I smiled back and said, "I am not ready to plant my roots just yet, as I have some unfinished business to tend to, but who knows, I may be back someday."

The trip to the airport took just under an hour. We had missed the rush hour, so it was an easy drive. Frankie pulled the limo up to the curb at Departures.

He opened the door for me and then proceeded to take out my two blue bags.

"Shall I take them in for you?" he asked. "No thanks, I am fine—I can manage," I said.

I had already shipped my trunk ahead, so I was traveling lightly. I paid him and gave him a generous tip.

He shook my hand and said, "It has been a real pleasure knowing you, Rose, and I wish you good luck on your adventure, and I hope to see you again someday."

I went through security, and I proceeded to the check-in area, where all the desks were all in a row, their overhead screens showing flights to Boston, JFK NY, Amsterdam, Hong Kong, Dubai UAE, Johannesburg/Cape Town, and the usual summer vacation spots of Madrid, Rome, Venice, and Malaga to name just a few.

I found my flight and proceeded to the check-in desk. Just a few people were in line. I was early, as usual; mostly business travelers for check-in I noticed.

I passed my ticket and passport, with all the necessary papers to the check-in clerk, and put my blue bags on the baggage escalator. I opted for a window seat, and as I was in business class, I assumed I would not have anyone in the next seat to me.

My hunch paid off, and I had the seat next to me empty. This was a long-haul flight, so I would have it all to myself for the entire flight.

I had taken a small carry-on handbag, with some books and writing materials, and of course aspirin and my travel socks, just in case I got a headache or leg cramp.

I took my jacket off, folded it, and placed it in the overhead bin. I had dressed business casual, in slacks and a blue silk blouse. I made myself comfortable and settled down for the long trip.

I had very little sleep the previous night as I was finishing packing up my home. I had rented it for two years (you always rent furnished I was advised; it's much easier to evict tenants this way, if the need arises). Hopefully not in my case, I said to myself as I crossed my fingers.

I had shipped all my personal items ahead, and the rest I had put in storage boxes.

My sister Lily was holding on to them until I decided where I would finally settle down.

I loved my home. I had it decorated in pastel shades, with lace curtains on the windows, but I especially loved my garden. It had all kinds of flowers and many roses; all my friends loved to sit out there in the evenings with me and smell the different scents. Already I was starting to miss all that. My neighbor Ellie had lace curtains too, and I liked them so much that I had similar ones hung. I had wonderful caring friends, always there for me if I needed them.

I had many friends, but Patricia I had known since childhood; we always called her Pat.

She was a tall, blonde-haired person, and had a wonderful caring nature. She worked as a paralegal, and I think she helped support her entire family. I never heard her complain.

Brenda was elegant, just like a model. She was a doctors' assistant and she lived the good life.

She was always flying off to exotic places for long weekends, yet I felt something was missing in her life. I had many more girl friends, but Pat and Brenda lived the closest to me.

The flight was not full, and after years in the airline industry, I could see why it was going through a tough time. High prices had reduced the number of flying passengers, but experts said it would rebound, but only time would tell.

The stewardess went through the usual safety procedures, and at last, the co-pilot addressed us, telling us we were second in line for takeoff.

The takeoff was smooth, and before long, we were airborne and on our way.

I never drank on a flight before, but this time I decided to have a glass of wine.

It was a South African red wine, and it tasted good. I guess I needed this to settle my nerves, and I kept telling myself that I was doing the right thing.

I put the 'Do Not Disturb' sign on my seat back, closed my eyes, and my thoughts drifted back to twelve years prior.

IRELAND 1966

THE GOLF TOURNAMENT

It was a beautiful morning, in early June, and the golf tournament was starting the following week. It was a pro-am tournament, with a large prize purse.

The CEO of the company where I worked, and who was also sponsoring the tournament, asked me if I would assist in the hospitality tent and greet the golfers at the dinner receptions.

A reception had been scheduled for each evening of match play, all except the last day.

I was going to be twenty-four next birthday, and considered a very pretty, highly educated, respected, and popular young woman, with no skeletons in my past.

I dreamed of meeting "Mister Right" and settling down and living happily ever after, but to date I had not found my soul mate.

Sometimes I questioned if there was such a person, or if it was just a myth.

I gladly accepted the CEO's offer, and I proceeded to call my hairdresser for an appointment the following Tuesday, the day before I was to greet the golfers.

The week leading up to the tournament was busy. I got a list of all the players and what country they came from. I read up on their records, and checked to see if any of them had special needs, like food, etc. I always did my homework before I hosted a function like this. They had come from all over the world, including the USA, Spain, Sweden, Australia, New Zealand, and South Africa, just to name a few of the countries.

I had done other sporting events, but this was my first golf tournament. I was very excited, as I had never been to any of those countries.

I was not a golf fan and did not play golf (women did not do this very much then, as women could not become a full member of a club).

I went shopping on the weekend and bought some new dresses. Blue was my color, so I bought two blue ones, and a blue and white one.

I just knew deep down that something special was about to happen to me. I had a special feeling all week long. I had dated several boyfriends, but no one special.

I kept thinking of Nana's words: "You will know when Mr. Right comes along." Nana was my grandmother on my mother's side.

My friends said I was too fussy. I just never felt that I had met the right one, just yet.

Wednesday arrived, and I decided to drive my own car to the hotel rather than accept a lift from my boss. I liked to be independent, leave whenever I wanted to, and not depend on others.

I had picked out a beautiful blue silk dress that I had bought over the weekend and matched it with patent shoes and bag. The dress matched the color of my eyes, deep blue, so I felt good.

I parked my dark blue VW as near to the entrance as possible, in a well-lit area.

I was much too early, but that was me; I was always early and I made straight for the ladies' room to check my lipstick. I never wore makeup, only lipstick.

I washed my hands and made my way to the reception room.

The room was empty with the exception of some waiters filling water jugs and lighting the buffet burners.

I checked over the tables, and they all looked nice. We had decided not to put place names on the tables, just leave it a buffet, with open seating.

I had two girls from the office helping me as well; both were older and married, so I did not have that much in common with them.

At 6:30 p.m., some folks started to arrive for the 7:00 p.m. buffet reception. Press, media, and a TV crew were already set up, so it was just a wait for things to get started. I was a little nervous, but I tried to look calm.

The golfers started to arrive, and I began to think about what kind of lives they lived.

Exotic places to play golf, adoring fans, beautiful hotels to stay in, and I guess no shortage of woman friends. It seemed to be a very glamorous lifestyle. They spent a lot of their time traveling, so home life must be difficult. I wondered how they coped with this and how their relationships stood up to the pressures. Yes, I wondered.

They arrived in groups of three and four, and they all seemed to know each other; I guess they all play the same tournaments. We had split them between three hotels in the area so that they were near each other. I made myself known to them as they arrived, and told them if they needed anything, I was there to assist them with my two colleagues from the office, both of whom had also arrived by this time. There were the usual speeches and accolades and lots of laughter before it was finally time to sit down to eat.

I waited until the end of the line with my co-workers, and then I put a small portion of food on my plate, I was too excited to eat, and the three of us looked around for a table to sit at.

We found a table near the back of the room and proceeded to finally relax and enjoy the rest of the evening.

The table seated eight, and four other people were already in their seats. We found out later they were all caddies. All the top-ten golfers were present, so it was exciting to see them in person. It never occurred to us to seek autographs; it was not the done thing, as we respected their privacy at all times, both on and off the course.

We had joined with the caddies in small talk, and answered whatever questions they asked about the area. Some had been here a few days already for practice rounds, with their golfer (some golfers always brought their own caddie), so they were already familiar with the well-known places.

Suddenly a voice said, "There you are, ladies. I wondered where you had gotten to." I looked up and there he was—tall, blonde-haired, very tanned, and stood about six feet or so, aged about twenty-six or -seven, I thought. I felt a shiver go through me.

"May I join you?" he asked.

We did have one vacant seat at the table, and next thing I know, he was sitting down beside me, as that is where the vacant seat was.

He introduced himself as Kedrick from Cape Town, South Africa, and he was with the tour. He was a professional golfer he told us.

We all introduced ourselves, and everyone got involved in the conversation.

He knew most of the other men at the table, the caddies, so he was joking with them, telling them that they had the best table in the room.

He insisted on ordering some wine for all of us, and we had a wonderful evening.

Before we knew, it was time to wrap up the event and say goodnight.

I wished him good luck in the tournament and that I would probably see him at the dinner, after the game next evening. We had a dinner planned for each night of the tournament, every night, except the last one, as they usually left for home, or they went on to another tournament, after their final round.

He looked straight at me and said, "Keep a seat for me, Rose." I just nodded.

I drove home that night and I just could not get him out of my mind.

I awoke very early, and I got up and made a strong cup of tea. I was not going to watch the players today; I had to go into the office to prepare some reports and charts for our annual sales conference the following week.

I showered, dressed, and went to work very early to get a head start on things.

I had my own office, so I often came early, and I had my own parking spot too. This was a real annoyance to several of my co-workers. They often asked why I had been allocated my own parking space. Well, the answer was I had to do bank runs each day and I could never find a spot when I came back; someone always had taken the parking spot I had parked in. I had planned to leave early so that I could get home and have some time to change before I joined the dinner party at 7:30 p.m. It was being held in the same hotel where we had last night's reception.

I worked really hard all day, and just had a banana for lunch, so I took no break.

I left the office at 3:30 p.m. and drove home, and I made some tea and a small turkey sandwich, as I knew it could be a few hours before I would eat again.

This time I wore a white Irish-lace blouse, with a black taffeta skirt, and finished it off with black accessories. The skirt had a red rose embroidered at the waist, and it looked very pretty.

I got to the hotel just before 7:00 p.m. and parked near the same spot as the previous night.

Once again, I went to the ladies' room, checked my lipstick, washed my hands, and headed for the reception area.

The clerk told me the dinner was being held in the ballroom, as they felt it was roomier than the original room I was told it would be in. I dashed to the ballroom to make sure all was in order, and it was just perfect. This time the tables seated ten, round tables, much easier to hold a conversation with everyone.

The two girls from the office (they had been given the three days off for the event) arrived, and we chatted for a while, and then the guests started to arrive. Again, it was open seating, but waiter service with a full menu.

I picked out a table right in the center of the room, left my bag and wrap on a chair, and proceeded to mingle with the crowd.

Pretty soon, the tables started to fill up, and then I heard my name called out.

I looked around, and there he was with about five other guys.

I immediately showed them the table I had picked out and I said, "Is this okay for you all?"

"Yes, this is perfect," someone answered, and we proceeded to take our seats.

I found out later that two were from Australia, and three were from England.

We had a pianist playing background music, and the song he was playing then was "Strangers in the Night." He played all the songs I liked. Was this an omen, I wondered.

The CEO of the company addressed everyone, saying, "The course played well today, so it looks like a very competitive tournament is on the cards," several people clapped, and he proceeded to say, "I hope the weather holds out for the rest of the week, now please enjoy your meal."

Our table was full at this stage, three girls and seven men—very interesting men, I might add. They had lots of funny golf stories and travel stories, and incidents that had happened to them, so I found it very interesting and amusing.

The waiter proceeded to take our orders. I ordered a prawn cocktail to start, with lamb cutlets for a main course. I very rarely have dessert. Kedrick asked me what would I recommend, and I suggested some ideas, and he looked at the menu again and said, "I will have what you are having."

He ordered wine for everyone (this was on a separate tab, so he told the waiter he would pay for this later at the bar). The house wine was free, but he said he wanted something special for a special occasion.

The conversation varied, and we all took part in it. The plan was to have all the golfers back to their hotels before 10:00 p.m. as some had an early tee time start.

As I prepared to leave, he asked if he could walk me to my car. I gladly accepted and I said goodbye to the others seated at the table; they were also making moves to leave as well.

I picked up my wrap and bag, and we made our way out to my car. He said, "Hold my hand," and he asked me for my keys to open the door. I hesitated at first, but then handed them to him as he held on to my hand.

He opened the driver's door, and then handed the keys back to me, and gestured for me to get in. Just as I was getting in, he touched my arm and pulled me towards him, and he planted a big kiss on my cheek.

"I really enjoyed tonight—are you coming to-morrow?" he asked as he looked into my eyes. I was blushing as I replied, "Not to the tournament, but I will be there for dinner."

Once again, he said, "Keep a seat for me."

Again, I drove home with him on my mind. I could not sleep that night; I just kept tossing and turning, until eventually I must have dozed off, because the next thing I remember is the phone ringing. I sleepily reached out for the phone only to find my dad at the other end.

"Did I wake you?" he asked.

"Not really," I said.

"I wanted to get you before you left for work as I know you leave early."

I looked at the clock on my bedside table and it said 7:00 a.m.

"What time will you get here on Saturday evening?" he asked.

What! Oh, my God, I had totally forgotten that weeks earlier I had promised to visit home this weekend.

"Dad, can we make it the following weekend?" I asked and I proceeded to tell him all about the golf tournament, and how I had been roped into the greeting and hospitality tent for Saturday and Sunday, and I also had to attend the functions each evening.

He sounded sad, but said, "That's fine, Rose, and don't you go running off with any of those handsome golfers now; you know most of them have a girl in every country they play in."

I loved my dad; he was everything to me: tall, dark, handsome, stood about six feet tall, but had some grey hairs appearing at his temples now.

I said, "Say hi to all at home and I will see you all next weekend, Saturday evening after 3:00 p.m. How is Mam—has she gotten over her cold yet?"

"Yes, she is fine," he answered.

"I love you," he said, and I answered back, "I love you too, Dad."

I got up, showered, dressed, and had a leisurely breakfast as I did not have to go to the office today. I decided to go to my club and swim a few laps. I was a longtime member here, and I swam at least twice a week for exercise.

I called my friend Pat to see if she would come join me, as she was off work this week.

She was unable to, as she had a doctor's appointment, but said she would meet me for lunch at 12:30 p.m. in a local restaurant.

The swim felt great; I was so full of energy when I met Pat, and we talked and talked until 2:00 p.m. until finally she said, "I have to go as I have to pick up my sister's kids at 3:00 p.m."

She took care of those kids as if they were her own. She would make a great mother someday.

I headed back home and looked in my wardrobe to see which dress I would wear tonight.

I choose the blue and white one with white accessories.

I put the plug in the bathtub and decided to have a relaxing bath before I left for the hotel.

I left the taps on full, and went back into the bedroom to get out fresh underwear, and I laid everything out on my bed.

I must have lazed in that bath for nearly an hour, fantasying about "suppose I did run off with a golfer"? I do not think they are like sailors, a gal in every port. Well, whatever, that is the saying anyway.

Is it true? Who knows?

I left for the hotel before 6:00 p.m. to beat the traffic. We had chosen a hotel on the waterfront for the last two nights' dinners. I had already checked out the place last week, so I knew exactly where to park, overlooking the bay.

I loved the water, and I hoped someday to live near it.

I pulled in, found a space, parked and locked up my car, and headed for the hotel lobby. The dinner was being held in the "Green Room." I did my usual trip to the ladies' room to check my lipstick and to make sure I was looking good.

Just as I was washing my hands, my two girls from the office appeared. They said some of the younger girls from the office were going to drop by later, just to look. They told me our boss had cleared it.

Again, I found a nice table near the middle of the room. This one sat eight people, and it was oblong in size. I prefer round tables, but you have to take whatever is on the hotel floor plan.

Kedrick and three other golfers arrived, and they came looking for us. We showed them the table we had kept for them.

The room started to fill up, and another golfer came over to our table. We now had a full setting, and Kedrick insisted I sit at the head of the table, and he sat to my right.

The conversation turned to the day's golf, and I found out that none of the golfers at the table had made the cut.

Someone said that it was a brutally atrocious day out there; the wind came from everywhere.

You teed up, and it was one way, and by the time you hit the ball, it was somewhere else.

Interesting item came up during the conversations and somehow it bothered me. Someone had asked Kedrick why he did not play in the USA. He very quickly replied that it was too dangerous as there had been death threats against South African players at that time.

What was that all about? I asked myself. I found out later it had something to do with South African politics.

They were all flying on to Spain on Sunday night to play in a tournament near Madrid.

Now they had Saturday and Sunday free, and they all wanted to see some sites, and party a little.

I told them I had to do the hospitality tent both days, Saturday in the morning and Sunday afternoon, but only if needed.

I did have the final dinner on the Saturday night to attend. Nothing was planned for Sunday, as most of the golfers went home or on to the next tournament on the Sunday evening.

The waiter came to take our orders, and Kedrick ordered some wine, and he chose the same dishes as I did; this time it was tomato soup for starters, and smoked salmon for the main dish. Again, we did not have any dessert.

At least we had that in common; we liked the same food, and we did not order desserts.

Everyone started telling stories, and again I found it so interesting listening to all their adventures. Some were funny, and some I would not repeat.

Time just flew by, and then the younger girls from the office appeared at our table.

I introduced them to everyone, and one of the golfers suggested we all go back to their hotel, as they had a disco there, and they had free passes. I hesitated at first, thinking I had a full day ahead, with the hospitality tent and the dinner, but Kedrick insisted I go.

We finished our wine, and we all left together to go to the disco. They all had free double passes, so no one had to pay.

We danced until two a.m., and it was just wonderful being so close to Kedrick. It felt so right dancing with him, and again my mind was wondering, what if...

I was driving, and I already had a glass of wine with dinner and that was my limit, so I just sipped a ginger ale.

Something just drew me to him; it was as if I had met him before.

Then it dawned on me; he had reminded me of my dad, when Dad was younger, same ways, same smile, no wonder my heart was pounding when I was with him.

He asked where I had parked my car. I showed him the way as we walked hand in hand back to the car. Music was still blaring from the disco, and "Strangers in the Night" was playing.

"May I have your keys please?" he asked; this time I did not hesitate.

He said, "May I sit in and talk to you?"

I said, "Sure, but I have to get home; I have an early start in the morning."

We sat, talked, hugged, and kissed each other, and he said he would drop by the hospitality tent around noon, and perhaps we could have lunch together, "Is that okay with you, Rose?" he asked.

I said, "Yes, I would love to," and we kissed again, and he got out of the car.

He told me to lock my doors, and he waited for me to drive out of the parking lot.

I could see him in the mirror and thought, *Oh man! How can this be happening to me?*

I was not prepared for this. I had never felt like this before.

I was just a hardworking girl that had never been out of the country, and never flown in an airplane. I was well spoken and I dressed nice. I was very well educated, but I kept asking myself the question: "Why did he pick me?"

I climbed into bed, and I set my alarm for 7:00 a.m. That gave me about four hours sleep.

It seemed like only a few minutes before my radio came on. I got up and had a quick shower, put the kettle on the stove, lit it, and took a muffin from the fridge.

I put the muffin in the toaster, and made a good strong cup of tea. I was not a coffee drinker; I had one occasionally, only if I could not get a proper cup of tea.

I had the daily newspapers delivered on Saturday and Sunday only; the daily paper was on my desk each morning during the week. I put blackcurrant jam on my muffin, and I sat down to read the paper, mostly the headlines. I did not feel like having cereal today as I really was not hungry, but I knew it would be late before I had lunch, so I had to eat something, and the muffin filled the gap.

I just glanced over the headlines to see if anything caught my eye, nothing interesting, so I turned over to the sports section, and I checked out the golf tournament results. All the usual top names were there, and only three strokes separated the top-ten players, so it looks like it is going to be a nail biter. I like a nail-biting finish, and the back nine is where you usually get one.

I decided to dress casual today, and I picked out a dress to change into at the hotel for the dinner that evening. I was going to watch the players on Sunday only, and only do the hospitality tent, if required, for breaks. I had already arranged this with Tom who was running the affair. Tom was our Commercial Manager.

I was not due at the course until 9:00 a.m., so I had plenty of time to get ready. I put my dress on the back seat of my car. I had picked out another blue one I had for a few years, but no one that was going to the dinner this evening had ever seen it before, and it was my all-time favorite.

I drove to the course, and I had a special pass to park behind the hospitality tent.

It was another beautiful day in the mid 60s, which was perfect, and of course, no humidity.

I walked into the tent, and immediately Tom, my colleague from work, called me over.

"Can you relieve me here for an hour or so as I have to run back home?" he asked. "My wife has locked herself out of the house and she cannot find the spare key. It is usually in the flowerpot, but it's not there." He said.

I was to discover much later that she had actually done this last week as well, and she had forgotten to put the key back in its hiding place. Cindy it seems likes her gin, but I do not think Tom was too supporting to her anyway. I heard the office gossip; some business trips were more than just business trips; rumor had it that he was linked to at least two of the female sales associates.

My feelings, well, in situations like this are "Live and let live, and to each his own."

It is not my business; it is their business, but I do not like to see people get hurt.

Most of the people that visited the tent were business people, all with free passes. They ate, drank, and took all the "freebies" that they could lay their hands on.

I even saw one woman take the floral centerpiece from the table. These were all well heeled, and I wondered, now why do they act like this? Well, whatever! They are who they are, and they have to live with themselves.

The morning flew by, and suddenly it was ten minutes to noon. I slipped into the ladies' room and reapplied my lipstick. The ladies' room was just an addition to the tent with one of those new portable flush loos. It was kept very clean, so I did not feel uncomfortable using it.

I came back out to find Tom, and to tell him I would be leaving shortly, as I was meeting someone for lunch.

I heard my name being called out, and I looked around, and there was Kedrick. I just loved his South African accent. He came over, put his arm around me, and kissed me lightly on the cheek.

I introduced him to Tom, and we chatted for a few minutes and then left.

"Well Rose, where to?" he asked. "Someplace quiet and overlooking the ocean would be lovely." Funny but those were my thoughts exactly, and I knew exactly where to go.

It was about a fifteen-minute drive, so we walked hand in hand to the car.

As I took the keys from my bag, he grabbed hold of me and kissed me full on the lips.

"I wanted to do that back there, but I did not want to embarrass you in front of your work colleague Tom," he said.

We both got into the car, and I started it up, reversed it out of the parking space, and left the golf course, heading for the coast road.

Neither of us had spoken since that kiss; finally, he put his arm around my shoulder and said, "Rose, will this bother you as you drive?"

"Not at all," I said, "we will be there in a few minutes anyway."

We pulled into the car park of the restaurant and found a space looking right out over the water. "This is beautiful," he said, and I asked him if it was like this in Cape Town.

He looked at me and said, "Any place is nice when you are with someone special."

I blushed and said, "That's nice." We sat a few more minutes taking in the view.

Some yachts were tied up at the pier and he said, "Let's walk the pier before we go into lunch."

I said, "Let's reserve a table first, and then we can go walking."

We walked into the restaurant and made a reservation for one hour later, at 1:30 p.m., and then we headed out to walk the pier.

We walked hand in hand, and he seemed very interested in the yachts; some were quite large.

I asked him to tell me about himself, and he said, "Not much to tell, Rose, but I want to know all about you."

I told him I was the eldest of five children: two boys and three girls.

My father is a builder, and my mother is a dancing teacher. I was convent educated, then I went on to do my degree in finance/accounting, and I was working as head of accounting in my present job.

My grandparents lived nearby to my parents' house, and Nana was my idol. I spoke to her every time I went home. She did not like phones, so only used it in an emergency.

She said she preferred to talk to someone while looking at him or her face to face.

I went on to tell him that girls did not do much else in those days except accounting or nursing, but deep down I really wanted to be a pilot, but girls were not trained as pilots then, although I did hear of a pilot's daughter applying to training school and it looked as if she would get in. I had not heard if they accepted her. I must check it out.

I told him I owned my own town home in the suburbs, with Dad's help of course, and I had no real serious boyfriends at this time.

"I was going to ask you if you had one," he said.

"Well, now you know, it's as simple as that, my life, and what about you?" I asked.

"As I said before, not much to tell. I always wanted to play golf, so here I am doing what I love."

He then stopped by a large yacht, and he looked all around it. "This one is real nice; my friend Barry has one similar to it. It's about eighty-five feet in length and I go out with him sometimes when I am home, which is not often nowadays.

"Barry is a Diamond Merchant, and we went to school together as children; he plays golf also, not professionally, but he travels with me sometimes when business permits. He has actually caddied for me once. That was such fun and we went on to win the game. I was thrilled and I told him he had brought me luck."

I said, "That's nice, but does his family mind him going off like that?"

Very quickly, he answered, "Barry has no real ties; his parents are dead, and he is an only child. They left him comfortably well off, or so he tells me, and he has even sponsored me earlier in my career."

He looked at me and said, "I hope you will meet him someday."

I said, "Kedrick, that would be very nice."

We continued to walk to the end of the pier, and then we headed back to the restaurant.

I still did not know much about him; he was not telling me anything.

We had a lovely table overlooking the ocean, and it was the perfect setting.

We both decided on something light as we were having dinner at 7:30 p.m. that evening.

I opted for a junior Cobb salad, and he had a prawn salad. "I love your Irish prawns," he said. "I could eat them every day; they are just great."

He asked if I would like some wine, but I declined. "It's much too early in the day," I laughed.

"I guess you are right, but we will have something special tonight." He said.

We had a real relaxing lunch, and both of us seemed very comfortable in each other's company. He asked if I was going home to change before dinner.

I said, "No, I have my dress with me; it's on the back seat in my car, and I thought I could change at the hotel."

He suggested that I go back with him to his hotel, I could shower and change there, and we could both leave for dinner together.

I said, "Sounds good, but are you sure your roommate Bob won't mind?"

He said Bob was at the tournament, and that he was going straight to the dinner.

Most of the younger golfers shared a room on tour.

It was just 3:00 p.m., when we left the restaurant, and dinner was not until 7:30 p.m., so I suggested we go for a drive on the coast road, known locally as the Tourist Trail.

He smiled and said, "Rose, don't you trust me to go back to my hotel with you so early?"

I said, "Something like that," and we both laughed.

"Maybe you are right," he said.

We drove, and stopped several times along the route to soak in the view and the scenery.

It was beautiful along the way. *Nothing like blue skies and blue-green waters to add to the romance of the day,* I thought.

Finally, it was time to turn back, and I suggested we go inland over country roads and past quaint little villages. It would take about fifteen minutes longer, but it was well worth it, and we did have plenty of time.

Some of the little villages seemed as if time had stood still for them. Children playing ball in the streets, women talking in little groups, but all the time they were keeping an eye on their children. Looking back, I think, my, oh my, how times have changed.

He was very silent for a long time, and then we spotted a little white chapel on a hill and he reached over to touch my arm and said, "Can we drop in there?"

I pulled over and we went inside; chapels were never locked during the day, so I knelt down and prayed that this day could go on forever.

He walked all around the tiny chapel, and then knelt for a few minutes.

I noticed a real sadness come over him, but I walked to the back to give him some privacy, and I waited. I even thought I saw a tear in his eyes.

We were back on the road again, and he was still silent when we pulled into his hotel.

It was just around the corner from where we were having dinner that evening.

I suggested I would drop him off and go park the car near the hotel where we were having the dinner, and walk back to his hotel. "I may not get parking there later on," I said.

He said, "No! No! I'll walk you to your car tonight, so just park here."

I parked, and I took my dress and shoes from the rear seat and headed into the hotel.

He picked up his key from reception, and I heard him ask if there were any messages for him.

"No Sir," answered the clerk, so we took the lift up to the fifth floor.

Just as we came out of the lift, his friend Bob appeared. Kedrick said, "I thought you were out on the course?" Bob answered "I just came back to change my shirt." I saw him wink at Kedrick, and he went on to say, "I am heading back to the clubhouse; we are all meeting there before dinner. Will you be at the dinner?"

"Of course I wouldn't miss it for anything; it's our last night here," said Kedrick.

We got to his room, # 525, and went inside. It was a typical two-bed hotel room, but it had a wonderful view of the ocean. I put my dress and shoes down on the armchair and stood looking out the window.

He came over, put his arms around me, and said, "Will you come to Spain with me tomorrow, Rose? We will be in Madrid for a week."

I so wanted to say yes, but I had commitments. I had the sales conference on Tuesday through Thursday, and I had promised Dad that I would go home on

Saturday, and I did not want to disappoint him again.

My heart was beating loudly and my head was in a spin. I took a deep breath and said, "I would love to, but I can't," and I went on to explain to him that I had commitments, and he seemed to understand.

He put his arms around me, kissed me, and said, "You go shower first," and he handed me fresh towels. I had a very quick shower, and I did not wash my hair; there was no hairdryer in the room.

I came out of the bathroom wrapped in the towel to pick up my dress. I did have my underwear on under the towel. He handed me my dress and said, "If you are finished, I'll go have my shower."

I said, "Yes, you go ahead."

He went into the bathroom but left the door ajar. I could see him in the shower and he looked so fit and tanned. I quickly dressed and did my hair, and when he came out, he had a small towel wrapped around him. I realized he had given me the larger one.

"Rose, you look beautiful," he said, "and you should always wear blue; it brings out the color of your eyes. In fact you look so good I could just stand here all night looking at you."

I smiled and said, "Get dressed; we have a function to go to in half an hour."

He came over to me and kissed me, and the towel fell to the floor.

I picked it up and handed it to him; he took it and went to pick up his clothes, and he went back into the bathroom to get dressed.

We walked over to my car, and I put my slacks, blouse, and walking shoes on the back seat, locked it up, and both of us headed, hand in hand, to the function.

I immediately picked out a table for us, and while Kedrick went to order his "special wine," I mingled with the guests and got the results of the day's golf game.

It was still anyone's game; only four strokes separated six golfers.

The game was scheduled to finish at 5:00 p.m. on Sunday (next day). Thunderstorms were forecasted, so the tee time was moved up by an hour.

Most of the golfers had flights booked that evening, and they were all going on to Madrid.

It was only a short flight, approximately two and a half hours, and it also gave them three full days to practice and recover before the next tournament.

I wish I could have gone along, but I guess the timing was just not right.

The room soon began to fill up, and I had to take the microphone to thank everyone and ask them to please take their seats as dinner was about to be served.

The tournament sponsor spokesperson then took over the microphone and went on to again thank all the participants for such a wonderful tournament so far, and looked forward to another good finish tomorrow, and also to see all of them again in two years.

I made my way back to my table. Kedrick was already there, and it was a full table with everyone seated.

He had kept the seat next to him for me. The party included the girls from the office, plus some of his friends. Some we had met the night before, and another Australian golfer that we had not met before.

It was a wonderful evening, great food, excellent wine, and lovely background music, and of course, the best company you could ask for.

The golfers still in the competition had already left before 9:00 p.m., but the rest stayed on chatting and drinking until 10:00 p.m. It was time! We picked up our bags, jackets, wraps, etc. and started out of the function room. We said our goodbyes, and it was sad, as we would probably never see any of them again, or would we?

Kedrick took my hand, and we headed towards my car. He asked me what my plans were for the next day. I told him that I had a pass for the course, and I had to be there for the presentation at 5:00 p.m. (that's if it didn't go to extra holes) so I would like to watch some golf, and I also had to pop into the hospitality tent to see if I was needed there.

He told me his flight was not until 9:00 p.m., and he had to check out of the hotel at 2:00 p.m., so he could meet me for lunch and he would like to spend the rest of the day with me at the tournament, and perhaps I could drive him to the airport.

I said, "That sounds great to me, and I would love to bring you to the airport; I was going to offer anyway." We arranged to meet at noon at his hotel.

He asked if I would like to have a late-night drink with him, but I told him I had a long day, and I was very tired, and would he understand if I just went home.

He said, of course, that it was very inconsiderate of him, but "I just want to spend every available minute with you." He kissed me goodnight, opened the car door for me, and told me to make sure all my doors were locked. I let down the driver window, and he kept his hand on my shoulder until I started to pull away.

I heard him say, "Sweet dreams, my perfect Rose, and always wear something blue."

It was well after midnight by the time I got to bed, totally exhausted, but I was a very happy girl.

I slept like a log, and awoke just after 8:00 a.m., late for me, and crawled out of bed and put my dressing gown on and headed for the kitchen. I put the kettle on and started to prepare breakfast, ham and eggs, as I was hungry. Did not know why, as I had dinner last night.

I had a nice leisurely breakfast, went out to pick up the Sunday paper from my porch, and I started to flick over the pages to see what was happening in the world today.

Same old stories—robberies, some terrorist group or other with allegations they did a bank every week to fund their cause, corruption in politics (does anything ever change), sex scandals, and the usual local stories and weather forecasts.

I headed for the bathroom to shower, and I took a long leisurely one, and I washed my hair, and just took my time getting ready. I opened my wardrobe to check what I would wear today, something casual, I thought. I found a pair of off-white slacks, and then I looked for something blue for the top. Finally, I found a nice cotton tee in royal blue.

I laid out everything, including fresh underwear, on my bed and looked for my white casual slip-on shoes; I needed something comfortable as I expected to be walking a lot around the course today.

I picked up the phone, called my parents, and chatted with them about ten minutes or so, and I told them I would see them on Saturday.

I think deep down I needed to do this, as I was afraid I might change my mind and take that Madrid flight, and it just was not the right time to do something like that.

I called my friend Pat and arranged to have dinner with her on Friday evening at her house.

I needed to talk to someone about my feelings. I put my laundry in the machine and went back to my bedroom to get dressed. I took out a wrap to have in my car as it would be another late night, and once the sun went down, it could get quite chilly.

I was to pick Kedrick up at his hotel at noon. He was leaving his luggage and clubs in my car as I was taking him directly to the airport after the presentation, and we planned to have something to eat at the hospitality tent before we left.

I locked up my house, and I decided to leave my laundry in the washing machine until I got back. It was risky leaving your dryer on when one was not there, my father's advice.

I drove to the gas station to fill up, and the assistant washed my windscreen.

I wish they would ask first as it is usually worse afterwards with slimy streaks all over it.

I asked him if he would check my tire pressure and he said, "Just pull over there when you are ready."

I tipped him and proceeded to drive away, looking forward to another beautiful day with Kedrick, but also remembering it would be our last—or would it?

I got to the hotel just before noon, parked, and went inside. He was at the reception desk checking out with some of the other golfers. I took a seat and waited for him to finish; he had not seen me yet. After he chatted with the others and finished his checkout, I saw him look around, then he saw me, a big smile coming on his face, and he came straight over to me and gave me a big kiss and a hug.

"Are you all set?" I asked him. "If so, I will bring my car around to the lobby and meet you there with your luggage." I went to get my car, and I drove it to the front lobby.

He loaded his luggage into the car, and we left for the course. I had a parking spot reserved for me at the back of the hospitality tent, so I pulled in there; it was also a safe place, as my colleagues could keep an eye on it. I was fully aware that I had his golf clubs in my car.

This was how he made his living, so I did not want anything to happen to them. I found out much later that he had in fact several sets of clubs.

We went into the tent, and I saw Tom and I asked him if he needed my help during the day.

He said, "We should be fine, and anyway you will probably be in and out all day."

We ordered two coffees and a small Danish pastry each, and when we finished, we went out on the course to follow the play.

One player had taken a three-stroke lead with nine holes to go, so the game was on with the last pairing teeing off at 1:00 p.m. We were silent most of the time, and then around 4:00 p.m. he whispered to me to go back to the tent to get something to eat.

We headed back through the trees and he said, "Rose, did you reconsider coming to Madrid with me?"

I said, "I gave it a lot of thought, but I do have commitments, and I really can't walk out on them." He held my hand and went on to say, "You know, when my coach Gary called me to take part in this tournament, I had said no to him. I hadn't played for several weeks, and I did not think I was ready.

"He told me that it was just what I needed right now, so to please re-consider it. I called him back two days later and said, 'Yes, I'll go to Ireland and Spain,' and it was probably the best decision of my life—I met you." I blushed.

He went on to say, "Rose, you have some of my mother's qualities. I have traveled a lot, to beautiful places, met some wonderfully interesting people, but somehow, you just caught my eye. You seem like the 'anchor' that brings the real world into focus, without any artificiality. So balanced, and yet, so down to earth. You are a perfect Irish Rose."

I felt the chills go right through me. I needed to pinch myself to see if this was a dream. Was he too good to be true or was he just a real good woman-izer?

"Rose, please hold my hand."

We got to the tent and we picked up a salad each, and then decided to sit under a tree to eat it. He also picked up two sodas, and we headed for a large shady tree away from the crowds.

I said, "Kedrick, I really know nothing about you," to which he replied, "As I said before, nothing much to know."

I asked him, "Why did you lay off golf for a few weeks?" He looked at me with some sadness in his eyes, and said, "A family member was very ill, so I needed to spend some time with them."

I did not push him any further as he seemed reluctant to talk about it.

Finally, the last hole was played at 5:00 p.m., just as we had hoped for, and it was a come–from-behind English player with two eagles in his last round that sealed it.

We hung around for the Waterford Trophy presentation, and mingled with some of the players.

For those who were going to Madrid, we had scheduled a coach to take them to the airport. Kedrick told Bob that he would see him at the airport, as I was giving him a ride there.

I did not have room for both of them, as the clubs took up a lot of room.

The golfers were being served a buffet in the hospitality tent, and shower facilities were available for them in the clubhouse before they left for the airport. I was told that some had stayed on in their hotel rooms to shower. I guess they paid extra for this amenity.

Kedrick and I left for the airport just after 6:00 p.m., and we drove the thirty-five minute trip (on a good day). We chatted all the way there about our four days together, and all the sites we had seen. He put his arm around my shoulder, looked at me, and said, "Rose, I would really like to keep in touch with you."

I said, "I was hoping you would say that, because I really enjoyed your company too."

He told me to drop him off at Departures with his luggage and then park and come back, and we could have a drink together.

I said, "Sure, but a coffee will be fine as I am driving, and I don't like late-night driving, so I need to keep a clear head."

We pulled up to the departures area, and he got out to get a trolley, and proceeded to put his luggage on it, two large cases and his clubs, which were in a leather golf bag case with his initials on it.

He said, "I'll be waiting inside for you, and don't take too long."

I found a space in section D not too far away from the pathway leading to departures.

I took my parking ticket with me, and headed back to departures. I went to the check-in desk for Madrid, and he was not there, so I looked around and then I heard his voice call me.

"Rose, I have already checked in, got my boarding pass, and my luggage is gone, so let's have that cup of coffee and sit and chat," he said.

We found a quiet table at the back of the café (as quiet as you could get in an airport café). Before I forget he said, "I need your address and home phone number, so that I can keep in touch with you. This is my phone number in Madrid, just in case you decide to change your mind," and he handed me a piece of paper with a hotel name and phone number on it.

I always carry a pen and notebook with me. I guess it is my accounting training, so I wrote down my phone number and address on it and handed it to him. (I wondered if he would really use it.)

He took out his wallet from a small holdall he was carrying, and put the piece of paper in it, and said, "Now, let us get that coffee. ... Are you hungry?" he asked. "Do you want something to eat?"

"No, I'm fine, but get me a cup of tea instead of the coffee; coffee might get me all worked up, caffeine wise, and it is getting late."

He smiled and went up to the counter and came back with one coffee, the tea, and an Irish scone. "I couldn't resist this nice scone, and you can share it with me," he said.

I said, "Okay, I will have a teeny piece." He went back to get a knife and another napkin and proceeded to cut me off a piece.

I wanted so badly to ask him about South Africa, but every time I brought up the subject, he very quickly changed the subject, so I let it drop.

The time flew and it was time for him to board his plane. All the other golfers had arrived by this time, and the place was a buzz with chatter and laughter.

He put his arms around me and said, "I won't forget you, Rose," and he gave me a long lingering kiss and then he was gone. He did not look back, but I thought I could see a tear in his eye when he kissed me. I stood around for a few minutes and then left for my car.

I felt so sad and lonely as I drove home in somewhat of a daze, because I really do not remember the journey until I pulled into my driveway.

We had bonded from the first moment we met, and I think I knew that "this is the man for me" when he first kissed me. It just felt so right, and I know he felt the same way, I just know, yet something was holding him back, what? Moreover, why had he chosen me? I had so many questions, but no answers yet.

I opened my door and headed for the laundry room, put my clothes in the dryer, and then checked my answering machine (a friend had brought me one from the USA). Just one message from an old boyfriend, the "on again, off again one," saying he would be in town the following Saturday night.

Good! I thought, I will be out of town that night, and I really did not want to see anyone for now.

The next week dragged by and the sales conference was boring; usually I enjoyed them, but I could not wait for Saturday to come; I was going to visit my parents.

Pat called me at the office Friday morning to see if it was still on for dinner that evening.

I said, "Yes, but make it something light." She said her brother had just brought over some fresh salmon so she would grill that and serve it with a salad.

"Sounds good to me, Pat, and I will see you at 7:00 p.m.," I said.

Friday evening I was not in the mood to tell Pat everything, so I just said I had met a real nice guy, and he said he would keep in touch with me. Time will tell.

Something kept me from telling her anything else. However, then there was not much else to tell.

I got up early Saturday morning and did my food shopping for the week. I did my household chores and changed my sheets. I loved white cotton, lace-trimmed sheets; only drawback, you have to iron them, but it is all worth it.

I picked up my newspaper and checked the sports section first. The results of the Madrid tournament were listed, and I saw that Kedrick had qualified for the final days.

He was in the top twenty, eight strokes back, but there was still two days to go.

He had not called me, but I guess he was busy.

As I did my chores, I kept thinking of Nana. She was my role model, and I was looking forward to seeing her today. I had some news for her.

I wonder what her reaction will be when I tell her the news; what will she say?

MY NANA, MY ROLE MODEL

Nana was my mother's mother, and she was probably the most important person in my life when I was growing up. She lived with my grandfather James just a few minutes' walk from our house. I spent time with her every evening after school, and she helped me with my homework.

Nana had been a governess and teacher to the local squire's family; she taught his three children. It was while she was working there that she met and fell in love with their groom James.

She told me it was love at first sight, but her family felt she could do better, so they forbade her to see him.

She could never get him out of her mind, and they met secretly over the next two years. He had by now been promoted to stable manager, so eventually her mother talked her father into letting them date, and they were given permission to date on one condition. The condition was that they would date for a year, and then if they both felt the same way about each other, then and only then, would they be given their parents' consent to marry.

Nana married her knight in shining armor fifteen months later.

They just celebrated their sixtieth wedding anniversary last month.

They were both in their mid-eighties and in poor health, but their memory was still as sharp as ever. I just loved to listen to their stories.

One thing Nana repeated over and over again was "Love always finds a way."

She taught me to respect everyone, even if I did not like or agree with them.

She advised me on how to dress suitably for each occasion. One of her sayings was "There is a time and place for everything."

Nana, her real name was Ellen, and James had two children: my mother and my uncle Pat. I found out much later in life that they also had twins, but they had died at childbirth.

She traveled as much as possible saying, "Travel is a great way to educate oneself; it broadens the mind."

She instilled in me the value of family, the need to give and receive love, to always believe in one's self, and to remain true to one's principles.

I loved Nana; she was my friend and protector. She was more like my mother than my birth mother was.

As I went through my teenage years, I felt I could tell her everything, things I could not tell my mother. She always listened, and then would put her arms around me and say, "Everything will be fine, just trust, and believe in your feelings."

Because of failing health and their refusal to go into a nursing home, my mother arranged a live-in housekeeper, named Cathay, to take care of them. They also had a nurse come by each day to make sure all their medical needs were seen to.

They were very happy with this arrangement, as it was their wish that they stay in their home, and die there.

My dad stopped in most days, just to chat, usually when he picked up my mother, who spent some time there each morning.

Nana treated my dad just like her son, and he loved her like a mother. His own mother died when he was just two.

My brothers and sisters always took turns to visit as well, so they always had company when they wanted it. Nana would be the first to tell you that she did not want company, so we accepted her wishes.

HOME SWEET HOME

I promised my dad I would be there before 3:00 p.m., and it was about a two-hour journey home.

I left about noon and started my journey. I needed to stop at the tobacco shop before I got on the highway as I always bought Dad his favorite tobacco.

He smoked the pipe and used Mick McQuaid plug, and every Christmas I bought him a new pipe. He liked the crooked shank type.

It was a nice day, no rain, so once again it was as if I was on autopilot for that journey.

On my many visits home, my first stop was to Nana's place. I tell her all about my life and my friends, and she always asks the same question, "Have you met your knight yet?" Well, this time I can tell her that things look promising.

I drove up the driveway, and I could see her looking out the window.

She always sat by the window, with the lace curtains drawn back, so that she could see whoever came up the driveway.

I knocked on the door and Cathay, the housekeeper, answered.

She whispered in my ear that my grandfather James had a bad night, and it did not look good.

I said nothing, just smiled at her, and said, "Just make sure he is comfortable."

Nana held my hand as I filled her in on my latest adventure, and she said, "Rose, I feel it in my old bones that this is your knight."

I smiled and said, "I hope so, Nana."

I spent some time with her, and I peeped in to see my grandfather, who was sleeping, so I just touched his head and left his room.

I said goodbye to Nana, and left for my parents' house nearby.

As I drove in the gateway, I could see my younger sisters playing on their swing set. One was twelve, her name was Lily, and the young one was four, named Violet. My mother liked flowers, so all her girls were christened after some flower or other.

They came running towards me as I always brought them something to wear and to eat.

This time it was tee shirts from the golf tournament, and some Cadbury's chocolate.

Dad and I were to visit his parents' grave that evening. He had broken his leg so could not drive, that is why he had wanted me to take him. Mam did not drive, but she was taking lessons from my eighteen-year-old brother. He was the best driver and mechanic around, or so he liked to tell everyone.

I wish I could be a fly on the wall when those two got together behind the wheel.

Dad said, "I have the kettle on for a cuppa before we go."

We all sat around the long kitchen table and had tea and homemade biscuits.

Mam said, "Don't eat too much, as I have a roast in the oven for dinner at 6:00 p.m."

She looked at Dad and said, "Will ya be back by then?" We both answered together, "Yes, we should be." We finished our tea and headed out to the car. I opened the door for Dad, and I got him seated.

He had crutches, so I put them on the back seat at an angle. We drove to the cemetery and it took about twenty minutes.

He hobbled along the pathway on his crutches and first stopped at his two brothers' graves. Both had died tragically at a young age within two years of each other.

One had drowned; he was just twenty-one. And one had a heart attack when he was thirty, leaving behind a wife and three children. Dad felt a responsibility to his family and he was always there for them.

He finally reached my grandparents', his mother's, and his father's graves.

He stood silent for a few minutes, and then I saw his lip quiver and in a broken voice said, "How will I know my mother when I die—I was only two when she died?" His father had only died last year; this was his first anniversary, and this is why he wanted to visit the graves at this time.

I am still haunted by his words, 'Will I know my mother?'

I remember my grandfather very well. We always spent three weeks at his house every year. Summer was usually a fun time. We had no school and no homework, so it was all fun, fun, *fun*.

All the grandkids that were able to cater for themselves spent the three weeks with him. He was not able to cope with younger ones, as he was not in the best of health.

It was a time I can look back on with much happiness. His house sat on top of a hill, and we all rolled down that hill; it was such fun. Sometimes if it had been raining, we were covered in mud. He so enjoyed seeing us having so much fun.

Dad walked or hobbled over to some other graves, neighbors and friends who had been buried there, and he spent a few minutes at each one.

Finally, he said, "Let's go home, and remember your mother makes a great roast, so we better not be late."

We arrived back just at 6:00 p.m. exactly and sat down to a lovely family dinner.

My two brothers had come back from soccer practice, so it was a full house.

It was to be one of those rare occasions, when all the family sat down together.

Family get-togethers are very important in my life.

We watched the *Late Late Show* on TV and I went to bed around 11:30 p.m.

I was tired, so sleep came quickly.

Mam and Dad always went to 9:00 a.m. Mass and dropped by Nana's house on the way home. I was to drive the others to the 11:00 a.m. Mass.

We got back from church just after noon, and Mam had lunch ready as I was leaving before 2:00 p.m. I did not want to be caught up in the weekend traffic on my journey back home, and I promised Nana that I would drop in to say goodbye.

I hugged everyone, and Dad came to the car with me.

He said, "Is there something you are not telling me; I notice you have a glow in your skin, and a sparkle in your eyes, what gives, and is it a *He*?"

I said, "Not really, I just had a wonderful time at the golf tournament, and I did meet a very nice South African golfer."

His mouth opened wide, and before he could say anything, I said, "He is tall, blonde, and very good looking, and a real nice person." I could see him relax, but I felt he was still concerned. Well, after all, it was a far-off country, and it was a very different culture.

I went on to say I would probably never see him again, but it was nice while it lasted.

He smiled and said, "I knew you had something special happen to you. You are glowing with happiness." *Was it showing that much?* I asked myself.

Nana was at her window as I drove in, and she just hugged me and said, "I'll keep you in my prayers, Rose," as I left to go.

I had an uneasy feeling that she was trying to tell me something. I waved to her as I drove out and said, "I love you." I hope she saw me.

I got back home just before 6:00 p.m. as I hit very heavy traffic on the way in to the city.

I found out later a big soccer game was being played that day, so traffic was heavy heading out from the stadium, which was not far from my house.

I did not feel hungry. I had a very big lunch at home, so I decided to pass on dinner, and I had some fruit and rice pudding instead.

I turned on the TV to see if I could get the golf results, but I guess I missed them. I would have to wait until morning to check the newspaper.

I had a quick shower, and put some milk on for a cocoa drink, and I laid out a suit for work in the morning.

I do not remember anything else until 6:30 a.m. the next morning, and when I awoke, I had to think what day was it, and then I realized it was Monday, back-to-work day.

I got up, dressed, and had breakfast, and headed to work where I had the daily newspaper delivered to my desk.

I went straight to the sports page, and I found the golf results.

Kedrick had finished in twelfth place. I thought, *His game is coming back; he must be good at what he does.*

My thoughts were racing all morning... *How come a well-travelled golf champion, who was constantly surrounded by beautiful people, stayed in posh hotels, yet he had picked me? Was it too good to be true?*

THE WAITING GAME

Another dull week at work, and no word from Kedrick… *Probably traveling*, I told myself.

He had not told me where he was heading after Madrid, so I assumed it was back to Cape Town. I remembered that he had not given me any contact number in Cape Town, only one for Madrid.

Two weeks went by and still no word. I did not know a thing about him, only his name and that he played golf, and had a friend named Barry, and lived in Cape Town.

Yet I felt this man was my "soul mate."

Would I ever see him again?

Three weeks later, I got a postcard from him mailed in Madrid nearly three weeks earlier.

It simply said, "Miss you, wish you were here. Love, Kedrick."

Well, it was something, and he did take the time to write it, which means he did remember me.

I had no contact number for him, so I had to wait for him to contact me.

Life for me had changed, and my job was becoming very dull, so I started checking out the employment section in the newspapers each Sunday.

I had a good job, but something was missing. *Maybe this too will pass*, I kept saying to myself.

It is now mid July, five weeks since I said goodbye to Kedrick at the airport, and I just had that one postcard.

My friends said, "Forget him. You have to start going out again; you haven't been out in five weeks, just snap out of this."

I arranged to have dinner with my out of town "on again, off again" friend on the last Friday in July. He would be in town then, playing a gig.

I had known Tim for years, since I was seventeen. He was a professional musician and singer, so he traveled a lot. He was a real nice person, but I did not feel anything that special for him.

He asked me what I had been doing, and I just replied that I had been keeping very busy with work.

I was relieved to say goodnight at the end of our date, and I did not invite him back home with me this time. I told him I was tired, and I just wanted to get to bed.

He was very understanding, and before going back to his hotel, he said, "Rose, I will ring next time I'm in town and perhaps you will be feeling better."

I said, "Yes, do that, Tim."

"MEET YOU IN PARIS"

It was now the first week in August, and when I got in from work on a Tuesday evening, my heart leaped when I picked up my mail. I had a letter from Kedrick.

I said, "Rose, calm down, count to ten, and just try to relax."

I opened the white envelope; it had no return address on it, but I knew it was from him, as I knew his writing from the postcard.

It read as follows:

My Dearest Rose,

Forgive the delay for taking so long to write to you, but I had a very busy schedule, and I was also moving house. I will fill you in when I next see you.

I will be in Paris last week of August playing in a tournament there, and I would love if you could meet me there. I will come a day or two early so that we can have a few days to see Paris together, before I start playing. I will ring you on Sunday morning, noon your time; you should have my letter by then, and you can let me know if you can make it.

I will send you a ticket, so please say yes. I have been thinking of you every day, and I cannot wait to hold you again. I just want to hold your hand tight.

Meet you in Paris, sweetheart.

With much love and kisses.

Miss you a lot.

Kedrick.

I could not sleep that night, and I made up my mind to go, even though I had no holidays or vacation time left until October.

"Yes, I will meet him in Paris."

I was in the office very early next morning, and as soon as my boss Norman came in, I told him I needed the last week in August off, as I was invited to a "party" in Paris.

He looked at me funny and said, "Would this party be tall, blonde, and plays golf?"

He went on to say that he had heard some rumors. "But I guess you would tell me if it was serious; you would, wouldn't you?" and he looked at me with a smile on his face.

"Of course I would," I answered and I stopped there.

I did not feel I should tell him anything more.

He said, "Go ahead, arrange it with HR, and see what they say. It's fine with me, just make sure you come back—you are badly needed here."

I just laughed and walked out and headed for HR. (*He guessed*, I said to myself, as I walked along the corridor.)

HR was not very nice when I told them; they had to reschedule some things, but they finally approved it until Thursday. I was to be back in the office on Thursday.

This is another reason I needed to move and find another job. HR was not very accommodating at times. The HR manager just did not make concessions to anyone.

I often wonder how he got the job. All he ever did was fix his toupee.

The days dragged by until Sunday morning, and the phone was by my hand all morning awaiting his call. At exactly noon, the phone rang. He was one hour ahead of our time.

I let it ring three times before I answered it. I picked up and I heard, "Rose, how are you?"

My ears were buzzing at the sound of his voice.

"I'm good, and it's lovely to hear your voice again," I said.

"Did you get my letter?" he asked.

"Yes, I have also cleared it at work to join you in Paris," I said.

"Rose dear, you have made my day; that's wonderful. Let me get my diary and check the dates. Can you meet me at Orly on Saturday morning?" he asked.

"Sure, I can be there," I replied.

"Okay! I will arrange the flights so that I can get there before you and meet your flight and we can travel to the hotel together." He went on to say, "I will overnight the ticket to you with all the details. I can't wait to meet you in Paris."

"Kedrick, I can only stay until Wednesday evening as I have to be back at work on Thursday morning. The tournament starts officially on Thursday, so you wouldn't have much time to spend with me then, and I figured it would be best if I wasn't there."

"Oh, I thought you could stay all week." There was a slight pause and then he said, "Rose, you know you are probably right, if I don't make the cut, I will be traveling back early anyway.

"Well at least we will have four days together. I cannot wait to see you, and see Paris together. Have you been there before?" he asked.

"No—never! I am looking forward to it very much," I said.

"Me too, I just passed through de Gaulle Airport once on my way to London, just a thirty-minute stopover. I saw nothing, just the airport, and so, it's my first time too," he said.

"Don't forget to pack something blue," he added.

We chatted for another few minutes, and he said, "I better go and book those flights and the hotel. You should have the tickets during the week."

"Kedrick, it's so great to hear your voice, keep safe and well, and I will see you real soon."

I was trembling as I said this.

"Bye."

"Bye! I miss you, Rose." He said.

Then the line went dead.

I did absolutely nothing for the rest of the day, just daydreamed.

Rose's dreams, yes mine, could be so romantic; I could not wait to meet him in Paris.

The following Wednesday I received the packet with my ticket and itinerary, and I began wishing the days would go faster, until I got on that plane.

I packed a small carryon case with two special blue dresses and some casual pants, a pair of shorts and some tops, underwear—just enough for four days.

I would wear my walking shoes, so packed my eveningwear shoes, just one pair that matched everything. I did not want to check luggage, as I just wanted to run off that plane as quickly as possible into his arms.

Well, I could always buy anything there, if I needed it.

FINDING LOVE IN PARIS

My flight was due in at Orly, Paris, at 2:00 p.m.; finally the big day arrived.

I parked in long-term parking, and then made my way to check in; it was approximately a two-hour twenty-five-minute flight, and I had to check in by 11:00 a.m. It was 11:30 a.m. when I got to the gate, and boarding was just starting. It was my first flight so I was a little nervous. I had never been on an airplane before. The few occasions I went to London, I went by ferry.

Children, and those needing assistance, were first in line for boarding. Soon, I was seated. I chose a window seat, and I settled down for my first trip to Paris.

A lot of butterflies and what ifs, supposing he is not what I remembered or was I just living a dream. All those thoughts were running through my head. My feelings and emotions ran between excitement and nervousness.

It was a pleasant trip, and soon we were preparing to land at Orly.

I came out the arrival gate, and even before I could look around, he was there, lifting me up in the air. It was just wonderful.

We hugged and kissed, and he said, "Let's get your luggage."

I said, "This is it," pulling my carryon closer.

"You are a clever girl," he said. "Likes to travel light. I like it."

We headed outside, and he hailed a taxi, and gave the driver the address of the hotel.

It took us about 30 minutes, and we pulled up in front of the most beautiful hotel I had ever seen. It was real Old World, covered with roses and clematis. He paid the taxi driver and we went inside.

I asked, "Where is your luggage?"

He said he had already left his luggage here earlier, as his flight had arrived several hours before mine. I suspected he wanted to check out the hotel to make sure it was up to his standards before he picked me up. I now know he has very high standards.

We went to the desk, and he had booked two adjoining rooms. I was relieved, but thought to myself, *I have a feeling we will not be using two rooms for long.*

It was an Old World hotel, but beautifully refurbished. We took the elevator to our third-floor room, which was also the top floor. Our adjoining rooms shared a balcony overlooking the Seine.

We also had to share a bathroom. Each room had a separate entry to the bathroom.

I felt like I had gone back in time. Kedrick asked, "Which room would you like?"

I said, "I don't mind." One was all white, and the other was a very soft yellow.

"You take the white one," he said, and he put my carryon down on a chair in there.

"I will have my luggage sent up," and he picked up the phone and told the desk to have the bellboy bring up his cases.

I took out my dresses and blouses and hung them in the old-fashioned closet.

It smelled of lavender. He sat and watched as I did this, and I put my wash kit in the bathroom.

A knock on his door got him to his feet, and he went to open it, but first gave me a kiss, saying, "Don't go anywhere, I will be right back."

He took in his cases, one small and one large, and of course, his clubs, in that nice leather golf case. He sat them down in a corner and tipped the bellboy, and closed the door.

He came back and said, "Let's admire the view from the balcony."

There was a little table and a couple of chairs on the balcony, just as you would see in a Parisian bistro, so we both sat down there.

There was silence for a few moments and then he said, "I have booked dinner for here tonight. I understand they have a nice restaurant downstairs.

One of the Spanish golfers had told me about this place. He stays here often. His wife had found it some years ago, while on a shopping trip to Paris."

"I was just about to ask you how you found out about this place. It's beautiful," I said.

He looked at me and said, "We should have an early night tonight as I have scheduled a sightseeing tour for the morning and a Seine dinner cruise for late afternoon, and I need to talk to you tonight and fill you in on my life."

"Do you have walking shoes with you?" he asked.

"Yes, I am wearing my comfortable walking sandals," I answered.

"Good. Let's freshen up and I'll unpack a few things. I have checked into a hotel on the golf course from Wednesday on, so I will only take out what I need for now," he said.

We decided to take a stroll along the riverbank and look at all the artwork and have a snack to keep us going until dinner at 9:00 p.m.

"They dine late here in Paris and you must be hungry; it's a long time till nine o'clock tonight," he said.

I freshened up and put on shorts and a tee; he did the same, and twenty minutes later, we were walking hand in hand by the banks of the Seine. We both looked the part of the tourist.

We stopped several times to look at the artwork, and we found a little café where we had coffee and a French baguette with a slice of ham.

It was a nice leisurely stroll, and before we knew, it was nearly 7:00 p.m., and time to get back to the hotel. I wanted to shower and change before dinner, and we did share a bathroom.

He said, "Rose, you go first as I have to make a phone call."

This time the hotel did supply a hair dryer, so I showered and washed my hair.

I put on a white terry robe, supplied by the hotel also, while I dried my hair.

He had knocked on my door, but I had the dryer on so I did not hear him, until he put his arms around me. "I did knock, and are you finished with the bathroom?" he said.

"Yes, you can go ahead," I said.

He went into the bathroom, and I continued to dry my hair. I went to change into my dress, the blue one, and I was all ready when he came out.

He was already dressed, wearing beige slacks and a short-sleeved pale-green shirt.

"I am being patriotic," he said. "Green for Ireland. Rose, you look impeccable, good enough to eat."

"Kedrick, you don't look too bad yourself, actually very palatable," I answered.

We both laughed, and I picked up my evening purse and we made our way down to the restaurant. It was on the ground floor, overlooking the water.

The waiter greeted us and took us to our table. A perfect picture by a large window overlooking the water; it was like something you would see in the old movies.

On the table was a single red rose in a crystal vase, white tablecloth, and silver tableware with crystal wine glasses. We looked over the menu, and Kedrick checked the wine list and ordered a bottle.

I knew nothing about wines; someone had once said to me, if you are not sure what to order, you cannot go wrong if you stick to French red and German white.

Kedrick seemed to know his wines. Everything he had ordered so far tasted good. Yes, he knew his wines.

I settled on pâté to start, and lamb cutlets for the main course. He chose a filet mignon, with salad to start. In fact, the whole meal was made up of several dishes.

Every time the waiter removed a plate, another was placed in front of us.

Small portions were on each plate, beautifully presented. What a wonderful tasteful collection of mouth-watering treats. I do not know what half of them were, but they all tasted good. Probably if I knew what some of them they were, I would not have eaten them. They say it's better not to know.

We talked, ate our meal, and drank our wine. I actually had two glasses, and then we had a liquor to finish the meal. Kedrick signed the bill, and we headed for our rooms.

He said, "Rose, let's sit out on the balcony and talk."

I slipped off my shoes and we went outside.

He held me very tightly and kissed me, and neither of us spoke for several minutes.

KEDRICK'S STORY

"Oh my dear Rose, I don't know where to start, but before you and I get anymore involved I need to tell you some things about myself. Please hear me out, and then we can discuss where we go from here."

Kedrick started to tell me the story of his life, a story I was eager to hear all about. He went on to tell me the following.

"I was born twenty-seven years ago in Rhodesia. I have one sister who is in medical school in Johannesburg. She is four years younger than I am.

"My mother died from breast cancer when I was just fifteen. My father died last year from a heart attack. I really do not have many close relatives; all my aunts and uncles are dead.

"I have some cousins in England and that is all. It is really just my sister and me.

"My grandparents came from England and they owned a very large ranch, and Dad took over the running of it when they passed. It was later taken away from us; South African politics is very messed up right now, and it is something I do not like discussing.

"We were compensated, but nothing like what it should have been.

"I went to a golf school after college as that is all I ever wanted to do. I stayed on in Cape Town after college. I had studied psychology and got my degree, but I have never worked in that field.

"I took a job at a very upscale golf club and worked very hard there to pay for my coaching classes, and I was able to play in some tournaments. I gave private lessons and earned extra money doing this, good money. I also had a trust fund to draw on if I needed extra funds.

"My parents had a trust fund set up for my sister and me after we sold the plantation.

"Soon I built up a reputation as a good golfer with a lot of promise; maybe I could even win the Masters someday. People had told me I had a lot of potential.

"I turned professional at age twenty-two. I was earning good money straight away, so life looked very promising. I was dating a girl from Cape Town; I met her at the club, as her father was a member there. We were dating for about four months when she told me she was pregnant.

"I told her I would marry her, and three weeks later, we were married. (I had never asked Kedrick if he was married. He wore no wedding ring, and I was to find out later most golfers do not wear rings as it can interfere with their grip. My head was spinning as I never expected to hear this, but I said nothing, and waited for him to continue.)

"We set up home in a three-bedroom condominium, and six months later, our daughter Hannah was born. She was just beautiful, but our marriage was just a sham. It was over before it began. We had nothing in common except our daughter.

"I was away most of the time playing golf, and I was earning very good money.

"I bought a nice house and put Sue (that is my wife's name) and Hannah there, but I kept my apartment, as I needed my own space.

"We kept up the appearance of a married couple for another year or so, and finally, we decided to divorce. Hannah was just three when the papers were ready to sign.

"I spent as much time as possible with Hannah, and I often wished that my mother were alive to see her, as she looked just like her. Two weeks before we were due to sign the final papers, we were told the news no parent ever wants to hear: Hannah had leukemia. Worst form they feared.

"I called my sister, and she told me she would research it for me. Weeks went by and it was test after test, but Hannah was a real trooper.

"I put my divorce, and my golf, on hold, and I was as supportive to Sue as I could be.

"My sister told me it did not look good as it was the worst form that Hannah had, and the prognosis was one to two years at best.

"Hannah was in and out of the hospital in Cape Town. I sold my condominium and bought another one near the water this past July. Hannah loves the water, so I take her there when she is able to come out for a day or so.

"I decided to do this after my trip to Ireland, and I saw how much you loved the water too.

"I was not meant to go on that trip, but my friends and my coach persuaded me to go as I needed a break, and it was time to get back playing golf again.

"There was nothing I could do for Hannah, and perhaps it would cheer her up if I told her stories about my trips, she used to like this.

"She is hanging in there, and even her medical team of doctors is amazed at her strength.

"She was so excited when I got back and brought her that Irish doll, that she told me to play more golf, and bring her a doll from each place I play.

"I said, 'Sweetheart, if that is what you would like me to do, I will do that for you.'

"I just play only about once a month now, if possible.

"Hannah is four now and still a real trooper. Treatments have taken their toll, but her doctors say her heart is very strong. Sue is coping by burying herself in the gin bottle; this was a habit of hers before anyway, but I am sure it is very hard for her too.

"One thing about Sue, she is a good mother. She adores Hannah and is always there for her.

"I do not want to finalize my divorce while Hannah is still alive. I never felt any need to rush it, but then I went to Ireland and found you. You just blew me away from the moment I saw you in that blue dress. You are the rock I was looking for; I need some stability in my life.

"Rose, my perfect Rose, that is my situation. I want you to have a good night's sleep, and it is now up to you to decide where you want this relationship to go.

"Our tour starts at 10:00 a.m., so we can have breakfast around 8:00 a.m."

I stood up, put my arms around him, and hugged him and he said, "Rose, please don't say anything now, just sleep on it, and I will see you in the morning. Just hold my hand for a moment."

He came over, kissed me on the cheek, and we held hands for a few seconds.

We both went inside to our separate rooms, and we went to our separate beds.

I just tossed and turned all night, and I wanted so badly to go to him.

I kept saying to myself that his marriage was over before I came on the scene, so do not feel guilty, and he is being honest and up front with me. I really like that about him, but all this has come as a great shock. This was the last thing I expected to hear.

Eventually I must have fallen asleep, but I was wide awake at 6:00 a.m.

I got up and showered very quickly as I did not want to wake him.

I dressed casual, slacks and blouse and my walking sandals, and I went out on the balcony just to sit and ponder. I heard him in the bathroom, and he came out dressed casual, and he came over to me and he put his arms around me and asked me if I had slept okay.

I said, "Eventually I fell asleep," and "How was your night?" I asked him.

He said, "I didn't sleep much. Let's go eat breakfast and we can talk there."

We both had a light breakfast, just tea for me, coffee for him, with some French toast. I had lost my appetite.

We went back to our rooms, and the door attendant said he would call us when the coach arrived for our tour.

I went to Kedrick, and I told him I would like to continue seeing him, if that is what he wanted also.

He said, "I was lying awake all night hoping and praying that this would be your answer."

We hugged, and he gave me a long, lingering kiss.

I told him I would not ask him anything about his life in Cape Town from now on, but that I was there for him if he ever wanted to talk about it.

He said, "I appreciate that very much, and you really are a wonderful thoughtful person.

"I am so lucky to have found you, and I never want to let you go—always remember that, Rose."

Then the phone rang, and it was the door attendant telling him the coach had arrived for our tour.

The tour took three hours, and it took us to all the usual sightseeing places in Paris; it was magical. I felt we belonged to each other. I just felt the bond as we walked and talked. I felt like I was on a cloud. It just did not seem real. Would I wake up only to find out it was just a dream?

The coach dropped us back at the hotel at 1:30 p.m., so we decided to go to a little bistro we had seen earlier near the hotel for lunch. We both felt so comfortable in each other's company, no secrets anymore.

We took a long time over lunch, and afterwards we strolled by the river until it was time to go back to change for our dinner cruise at 7:30 p.m.

I said, "What do I wear on this cruise?"

He said, "You looked so good in that blue dress last night, why not wear it again, and Rose, you go ahead and take the bathroom first, while I make a phone call."

This time I knew whom he was calling; it was the hospital to check on Hannah's condition, and I thought "it must be hell for him" and my prayers are with him and his family at this difficult time in their lives.

I finished in the bathroom and called out to him "it's free," and I went to my room to dress.

I put on fresh underwear and slipped into my blue dress.

I sat down at the dressing table to apply my lipstick. I never wore makeup, only lipstick, so it does not take me long to get ready. He had commented on this, about how fresh my face always looked, back in Ireland. "I guess it's the Irish rain," I had replied.

"I could never figure out why girls piled on so much makeup on their faces, really all they need is a good moisturizer at night.

"Some girls look so false with all that makeup. It could be interesting to check on them in thirty years or so and see the results of years of heavy makeup.

"I found a very good moisturizing lotion that I have used all my life. Recently I discovered a new one, and it is just as good; it is called CeraVe.

"It certainly works for me, and I know it is still on the market after all those years, so I guess it must be popular."

I found a radio by the bedside locker. I had not noticed it there before, and so while I waited for Kedrick, I turned it on. Elvis was singing, oh how I love his voice; it is so pure. His music will never go out of fashion; it's going to last forever.

I had closed my eyes to listen to the words when I felt Kedrick's arms around me.

"Do you like Elvis too?" he asked. "I listen to him every chance I get," I said.

"Good! We have that in common too," he said.

"Rose, you look real good, and I better not kiss you now as I would spoil your lipstick, but I will make up for it later," and he laughed, and he gave me a big hug.

I loved to see him laugh. His smile reminded me of my dad's, comforting and friendly.

We had to walk about fifteen minutes to where we joined the cruise.

"Let's take our time," he said. "I see you are wearing heels. Do you want to take a taxi there?"

I said, "No! I am fine; a taxi would not take such a short trip anyway, and if they did, would probably charge an arm and a leg for it."

We strolled hand in hand and came to where we were to board the cruise ship; actually, it was a large yacht, and it was moored alongside the Seine.

It limited its passengers to forty, so it was a small intimate dinner cruise.

Background music was playing as we boarded and again that number came up, "Strangers in the Night." It seems all the oldies that I liked were being played.

He said, "It looks like this tune is becoming our anthem; we seem to hear it everyplace we go. I wonder, is there a message there?"

"That's nice, Kedrick, every time we hear it when we are not together, we can just close our eyes and pretend," I said.

"That's what I love about you, a true romantic. My mother was like that too, and you remind me of her sometimes." He said.

We wined and dined, and there was a small dance area onboard, so we just were swept away in each other's arms on the dance floor. He could dance.

All too soon, it was 10:30 p.m., and the yacht was heading back to dock.

We disembarked and started to walk back to our hotel, and I decided to take off my shoes and walk barefoot. There was a nice grassy patch alongside the footpath, so I was able to walk most of the way on that.

"Do you want me to carry you?" he asked. "There might be dog poop."

"No, no! I just love to feel the grass on my feet and it will be another special memory to have," and I squeezed his hand tightly.

We both stopped and he picked me up, kissed me, and said, "Rose! We will have many more special memories."

I said, "I sure hope so, lots more."

It was after 11:00 p.m. when we got back to the hotel, and we were both tired but very happy.

We did not need two rooms that night. We fell asleep in each other's arms, having made love for the first time.

I was awake early again, but I just lay there watching him breathe in and out.

Finally, he opened his eyes and said, "I thought it was a beautiful dream, but it's real."

We just hugged each other, and we lay there for a long time.

I said, "What plans do you have for today?"

He replied, "We can do whatever you want, perhaps visit the Louvre, Eiffel Tower, and just sightsee. Or have you any suggestions?"

I said, "No, let's have breakfast first, and then we can spend the day looking around and taking in the sights, just as you said, that sounds good, aah!"

We got up, again I showered first, and dressed in shorts and a tee shirt, and before I had my hair done, he was ready, so he waited until I was finished with my hair, and then we went down for breakfast.

There was a stand with various tourist-attraction leaflets in the lobby, so we looked through them, and he picked out a few to discuss over breakfast.

We decided on the Eiffel Tower and Notre Dame Cathedral, and we could have dinner at the hotel again that evening. We really liked it there, and we both felt it was a very romantic setting. It had a special attraction to both of us. It was as if we had been here in a previous life.

We finished breakfast and went back out to the lobby.

"What about a show tomorrow night?" he said.

"That sounds great," I replied. "What's on?"

"I don't know, but let's check at the desk," he said.

The clerk recommended a musical review dinner theatre, so we booked the tickets with dinner included. We went back to our rooms and I picked up my purse, and we headed back out to see Paris, this time on foot.

The Eiffel Tower was magic, and he said, "Some-day I will bring you back here when I am free to tell you all the things I want to tell you; it's not the right time yet," and he hugged me very tightly and gave me a big long kiss.

We had another wonderful day, and we had a light lunch at a very nice café, with French bread, cheeses, and coffee.

The tea was not too good in Paris. I do not think they boil the water, nothing like a good cup of Irish tea made with boiling water; coffee it will have to be until I get home.

We walked hand in hand back to our hotel, and both of us just collapsed on my bed.

We just lay there wrapped in each other's arms for at least half an hour or so.

I said, "Kedrick, I think we better change for dinner as it's 7:30 p.m. and I need to freshen up first."

"Yes, you go ahead as I need to make a phone call first," he said.

I was in the bathroom, and I could hear his voice in the background, but I could not make out what he was saying, I did not need to know.

I decided to wear dress slacks and a silk shirt to dinner.

I wanted to keep the other blue dress for the dinner theatre the next night, our last night.

He came back to my room just as I slipped into my slacks and he said, "I will have a very quick shower and be right back, so don't go anywhere, my lovely Rose."

"Fine, we have plenty of time and we don't have to go out anywhere, just downstairs, so take your time," I told him.

He was back in less than fifteen minutes in his briefs, and pulled on his slacks, and a very colorful shirt and said, "Okay, let's go, but first I have to do something."

I looked at him as he came over to me, and he held me so tightly I thought my ribs would crack. He kissed me and said, "You are my perfect Rose; I don't want this moment to ever pass."

I just held him and said, "I will remember this moment too; it's very special. Okay! Let's go as I am hungry, for food, right now," I said and we both laughed, and we went downstairs to the restaurant.

We had the same table, but this time we had a beautiful cream rose in the crystal vase; I think it's called a "Tea Rose."

I leaned over to smell it, and he had done the same thing, so we bumped heads.

We both could not stop laughing until the waiter said, "It must have been a good joke?"

Kedrick said, "This is no joke; it's the real thing, my friend."

The waiter looked puzzled, and he just handed us the menus, one each.

We ordered duck and lamb, and again it was beautifully presented. (I love French cooking.) It is always so delicious and looks appetizing and so tastefully presented.

We had some really nice wine. I said, "Write down the name of this wine for me. I must look for a bottle when I get back home, and every Saturday night I will have a glass to make a toast to you."

"There you go again, my romantic Rose," and he laughed.

Oh! It was so good to hear him laugh.

After dinner, we sat out on the balcony just talking and taking in the view.

"What will we do tomorrow?" I asked.

"Well, let's see, we have the dinner theatre tomorrow night at 7:30 p.m., so we are free all day. I need to do a little shopping; I have to find a little French doll for Hannah," he said.

"That sounds good to me as I like dolls also, and antique browsing is a hobby of mine too," I said.

We decided where to go the next day and he stood up, came over, and put his arms around me, "Let's go to bed—yours or mine?" He asked.

"Those beds are not very big; next time we will request a king size," he said.

Soon we were snuggled up in my bed, and that is how we fell asleep.

We both awoke at the same time; it seems something outside had awoken us.

We got up to look out, and some guy was serenading outside a house down from the hotel.

I said, "Seven o'clock in the morning?" He laughed and said, "It's nice anytime of the day or night to have someone to serenade to—now, why didn't I think of that!"

"Can you sing?" I asked.

"Oh yes, just like the Beatles," he answered, and then went on to say, "How I wish I could sing, of course, I could always hire someone to do it for me."

"It wouldn't be the same," I said, "so you better start taking lessons," and I started to laugh.

"Do you like the Beatles?" I asked.

"They are great, and I have nearly all their records. If they stay together, we can go to one of their concerts. I hear rumors that they may split. Let's put that on our calendar too," he said.

We showered together that morning and got dressed, again in shorts and tees, as it was forecasted to be another warm, hot day.

We had a good breakfast, as we did not know how the day would unfold.

We asked the girl at the front desk if she would recommend a nice shopping area where we could buy a doll and browse around some antique stores. She recommended two areas for us to try, so we headed off in that direction.

We found some really quaint stores, and I found a clock store. I said I wanted to take a look inside, as I loved clocks.

My father had once said to me "a ticking clock is the heartbeat of a home," so I have clocks everywhere. It can be a real pain when the hour goes back or forward; you know, spring forward, fall back. Then I have to change all of them.

"Now every time I hear a clock tick, I'll remember what you said; you have the cutest sayings," he said.

"Do you see anything you like?" He asked.

"Not really, and I'd have to carry it through Customs, and I only have a small case," I answered.

Finally after hours of strolling around, and after we had eaten a light lunch in a very pretty little café, nestled amid the shops, we came upon a doll boutique, so many beautiful dolls, and one little eight-inch "Pink Lady" in a cream lace gown with hat to match caught my eye.

I asked if I could pick it up and the assistant said, "Oui."

It was beautiful, and Kedrick saw me with it and said, "She's lovely—delicate, just like you."

He had found a very pretty French doll for Hannah, about the same size as the one I was holding.

He said to the assistant, "Please wrap them both for me, in separate boxes."

I started to protest, but he said, "My gift to you. When is your birthday?"

I said, "October 9th, a Libra, same as John Lennon's (The Beatles)."

"Well, take this as an early birthday present," and he held my hand as we waited for the girl to wrap them.

When we came outside, I asked him when his birthday was and he said, "19th of December." "Sagittarius," I said.

"Are you into that?" he asked.

"Not really!" I said. "But I do believe in telepathy."

We started back to the hotel because it had been a long sticky day, and we both needed to shower and change before the taxi was to pick us up to take us to the dinner theatre at 7:00 p.m.

We both had quick showers and got dressed for the theatre.

I wore my other blue dress and again he said, "You look lovely, my perfect Rose."

We had a really enjoyable night at the dinner theatre, but deep down, I was a wee bit sad.

It was our last night together, and I did not know when or if I would ever see him again.

He did not talk much on the way back in the taxi to our hotel. He asked if I would like a nightcap, and I said, "No. Let's just sit outside on the balcony for a while."

"Let me make a phone call first, and then I'll be right back," he said.

He came back, sat next to me, took my hand, and said, "Rose, this has been the most wonderful four days for me; I hope you enjoyed them too."

I stood up, kissed him, and said, "I'll always remember our first real date in Paris."

"Me too," he said, "and I promise you we will come back here someday, real soon."

He picked me up, and we went inside and lay on the bed. We undressed each other and just lay in each other's arms and made love.

"There is no need for you to come to the airport with me in the morning; my flight is not until 11:00 a.m., and you have had no practice rounds in before the tournament, so I'll take a taxi from here, and you go to your hotel, and perhaps get in a round or two," I said.

"Ever-thoughtful Rose," he said. "I would really like to take you, but if you are sure you can manage it, I would like to get in some practice."

"No problem," I said, "and we can have a nice relaxing breakfast and take it from there."

"Do you have any vacation left?" he asked.

"Actually I do have a week in October, and that's it until spring," I said.

"When in October?" he asked.

"It's the second week, my birthday week, I usually take it off," I said.

"I think I have a tournament that week in Granada, Spain, let me check in the morning, but let's get some sleep now." He rolled over to kiss me, and he nearly fell out of the bed.

We both fell asleep with a smile on our faces. We really do need a bigger bed.

Dawn came early, and I crept into the bathroom to have a shower before he awoke.

I was as quiet as possible, and I came out in the white terry robe and sat at the side of the bed just looking at him.

When will I see him again? Is this a dream? Will I wake up and discover it was just a dream?

Soon, he opened his eyes and said, "Good morning, have you showered already?"

"Yes! I just want to spend every moment with you until my taxi comes," I said.

He was up, showered and dressed, while I was dressing in my travel slacks and blouse, and then he said, "Now let's check my schedule."

He went to his small case and took out a diary. "Wow! That's brilliant; it's the same week as your vacation, I mean the Granada Tournament—will you meet me there?" He asked as he came over to where I was standing.

He picked me up and hugged me, and gave me a kiss. "You will come, Rose, please say yes?" he said.

I answered, "You just try to keep me away."

"I'll make all the arrangements, and I will send you your ticket, and you can check out things we can do there. We can do the same as here, meet on the Saturday before, but please stay the full week this time, please, please," and he had that look in his eyes—how could I say no?

"Sounds perfect, I'll do that," I said.

"There! It's all settled, now I don't feel too bad letting you go, as I know we have definite plans to meet soon again."

He held my hand and said, "Let's have breakfast." After breakfast, we made our way back to our rooms where I checked to see if I had packed everything.

I was going to carry my doll in a nice carrier bag the shop had provided.

I left my case at the door, and he came in and said, "We still have some time before your taxi arrives; let's just sit on the balcony and soak in the view again. I promise you, Rose dearest, I will bring you back here."

All too soon, it was time to go to checkout, so he got his luggage and called the bellboy to have someone come get it. He held me in his arms and again said, "I don't feel too bad saying goodbye, because I will see you again in less than six weeks, and I will call you at least once a week."

I said nothing, just smiled, and held him close. We kissed and hugged and then we went downstairs for my taxi; he was also leaving at the same time in his taxi to go to the golf course and get in some practice rounds, so we had ordered two taxies.

My taxi was on time; he put my case in, and came over to the open door with me and kissed me again. I sat inside, and I said, "I'll be waiting for your call."

I felt very happy and content on my way to the airport, and in my mind, I was already planning our trip to Granada.

The weeks flew by, and Kedrick did phone me several times a week, as promised.

GRANADA

Soon, it was time for my trip to Granada, and it was time to pack my case, a little bigger this time around. I headed out for the airport with my ticket in my hand (which had arrived about two weeks prior) and looked forward to the trip and meeting Kedrick again.

He met my flight, and he had rented a car, so we headed straight for our hotel.

We had the most wonderful time in Granada, and we visited the Magic City of Alhambra.

This is where Ferdinand and Isabella lived, and I understand this is also where she gave Columbus the funds for his trip to the "New World."

The gardens were beautiful, and the palaces were something else to see.

Kedrick qualified for the final two days golf, so I kept away from the golf course during the day, and I just went shopping and browsing around. He asked me to pick up a Spanish doll for him, so I did this, a very pretty one. (I knew what he wanted since our trip to Paris.)

We met up after he finished each day, and we had a lovely dinner and just one glass of wine each—after all, he was working, so he had to keep a clear head.

I went to the club on the final day as he was in third place, but I kept out of view and I had arranged to meet him outside the clubhouse, one hour after he finished.

This gave him time to shower and finish his business at the club.

We had checked out of the hotel before his tee time earlier that morning, and I had the car for the day. I was able to drive around and take in some sights before I headed back to the golf course.

We headed straight for the airport. My flight home was one hour ahead of his, so we went directly to the check-in desk for my flight, and then went to check him in.

He sat with me at my gate until it was time to board, and he gave me a big hug, kiss, and said, "I'll check my schedule and call you." He reached out to hold my hand and looked me straight in the eyes. Our eyes just met, and I felt weak. *Wow!*

"Thanks for being here, and you are the perfect rose." He said.

Again, he kept his promise, and he phoned me every week.

His next tournament was in Sweden, but I had no time left, so I had to pass on that trip.

He was coming to Scotland in early December, so I promised to meet him there for the weekend.

It was for some kind of golfing seminar, Friday to Sunday, at Gleneagles.

For the next six months, we met three times: the weekend in Scotland, and a weekend in Portugal, and one in London, in early March.

Again, we were so comfortable in each other's company, and it felt as if we had known each other all our lives.

We had a very funny incident in Scotland. We had gone in to dinner, and the waiter came to take our order. Kedrick asked him for any suggestions or recommendations.

The waiter said, "Yes sir. The haggis is very good tonight," and I saw him wink at the other waiter.

Kedrick looked at me and said, "Will you try it?"

"Do you know what it is?" I asked.

"No! I never heard of it," he said.

Then I started to laugh and said, "I think you better order something else, dear."

I explained it to him later.

In Portugal, he asked me if I could take a two-week vacation in April and come to Cape Town. He would like to show me around, and see if I would like the place.

I told him I would arrange it with HR as soon as I got back.

He then mentioned Hannah and said she was hanging in there, but they did not expect much longer, maybe six months maximum.

"Kedrick, only the man above says when, so think positive," I said.

"Rose, you are the one that's helping me through this, just by being here for me. You and my sister, she is great in keeping track of Hannah's treatments, etc., and making sure she is getting the best ones available." He gave a big sigh as he said this, and I could see a very distant look in his eyes.

Our weekend in London was just magic. Again, he promised me that we would come back there and see all the sights we missed on this trip.

"We will come when the weather is a little warmer," he said.

This was not a golf tournament, but a convention for golfers. The manufacturers sponsored it. Anything you needed for golf was on display there. I think Kedrick just came as an excuse to meet me. At least I hope so.

I found it very interesting, and I met some English golfer friends of Kedrick's.

I kept busy at work, and I went to visit my parents every month (just to have my mother's roast, not really!). I kept Nana in the picture, and she was delighted that things seemed to be working out for us. "I cannot wait to meet him sometime," she said.

I enjoyed the break from the city. I loved to spend time with my sisters and brothers, and Dad was always open to talking about whatever you wanted to talk about.

Dad was a little apprehensive about my trip to Cape Town. "You take care now," he said.

My mother usually got her say in too; she could talk to you on any subject under the sun.

Our family home was a large comfortable house on ten acres of property, with brooks, and streams, and woods. I loved to ramble through the woods.

Kedrick called to say my ticket for Cape Town was on its way, so now I was excited. He also told me to pack something warm, a sweater or jacket, as it can be windy and cool in the evenings.

CAPE TOWN

The big day finally arrived, and I had bought some new clothes for my trip.

It was a long flight, and I could not sleep, as all I wanted to do was see him, and hold him.

He was there to meet me, and told me he had put me up at the hotel in the same complex as his condominium. "I hope you don't mind, as I feel it's not the right time to have you stay in my condo. The hotel is also on the waterfront, so I think you will like it there." He said.

"I fully understand, and I would prefer it this way, for now anyway," I said.

We spent every day together for the first week, and he stayed over at my hotel at night with me. He took me to all the tourist attractions and some "off the track places." *I could like it here*, I thought to myself, *but I do not know anyone other than Kedrick, and I guess the time is not right for him to introduce me to his friends*. After all, he is still legally married. One afternoon he took me to a very pretty seafood restaurant. It sat just up from a beautiful sandy beach, so after our meal we walked along the beach. I remember looking back and seeing our footprints in the sand and thought how much in sync we were. Was this a good omen for us, I wondered.

Barry who owned the big yacht docked nearby did drop by the hotel one morning, and stayed with us for lunch. It appears that Kedrick had told Barry all about me.

He asked us out on his yacht that weekend, and we both looked at each other and Kedrick said, "Would you like that?"

I said, "Yes, I'd love it."

We arranged to go on Friday evening, stay onboard, and return on Saturday evening.

I was leaving on Sunday to fly back home. I did not want to think about this just yet. I was so happy here with him.

We had another lovely week; I saw a lot, and I did like what I saw. People were very friendly and polite and very well dressed, and I liked the fashion.

On Friday morning, Kedrick asked me if I liked Cape Town.

I said, "Yes, I really do." He hugged and kissed me and said, "I'm so glad."

Just then, a porter came looking for him, saying, "Sir, you have an urgent phone call."

He came back in about twenty minutes, and I thought he looked troubled.

I asked, "Is everything all right, Kedrick?"

He said, "Yes, but that was my sister, and she is in town tonight, and she wants me to take her to see Hannah."

I said, "You go. I'll be fine here."

He said, "Let me ring Barry and see if he can come by early and take you out." He called Barry, and I heard him say, "I really appreciate this, my friend."

Kedrick left late afternoon to pick up his sister, and Barry came to pick me up.

A woman friend, who was introduced to me as Ruth, accompanied him.

He said, "Pack an overnight bag, and I will have you back here tomorrow afternoon to meet up with Kedrick."

THE YACHT

We had a lovely cruise, with a picnic hamper for dinner and a few bottles of wine.

Both Ruth and Barry were very talkative; they asked me many questions about life in Ireland and what I did for a living.

Ruth mentioned she had visited Killarney once with her parents when she was a teenager and that she loved the place. "Actually, we have a Killarney here, north of Cape Town, never been there, but one day I will try to get there—near, but so far away," she said with a distant look in her eyes.

I guess she really did enjoy that trip to Killarney.

We wined, dined, and talked until midnight, and finally I said I would go to my bed.

This yacht had three bedrooms, all with private shower and toilet. Barry had shown me mine earlier, so I went straight there, having said goodnight to them.

I washed and freshened up and took my time and then I realized I had left my purse up on the deck. My pills were in it, and I needed to take one before I went to bed.

I was in my nightdress, so I crept up very quietly to get it. I did not want Kedrick ending up with another unplanned baby.

Barry was sitting alone at a bench. I guess Ruth had gone to bed also.

He had a box of golf balls beside him. I hesitated, as I did not want him to see me in my nightdress, so I kept very quiet and watched him for a few minutes, trying to get up the courage to ask him to throw me down my purse.

Then, I could not believe my eyes. He unscrewed a golf ball; it came apart and out fell diamonds. Then, he did another and another. The inside of the golf balls seemed to be lined with foam, and the diamonds were inserted in little slits in the foam.

What was going on? I suddenly felt scared, and I went to go back to my room.

He looked up, and he seemed to listen, as though he heard something.

I kept very still and waited until he went back to whatever it was he was doing, and then I slipped back to my room.

I lay awake all night thinking, *Was he smuggling diamonds?*

I remembered Kedrick telling me he was a diamond merchant, but I still felt scared.

It was all so weird. Was Kedrick aware of this? Was he involved also? Was he too good to be true? I knew nobody here, so what was I to do?

I remembered my father telling me that he had read somewhere that diamond smuggling was common in Africa. They used the funds to finance guerrilla warfare, and other illegal activities.

I think he mentioned that they called them blood diamonds.

I was frightened, and I was in a strange land and, really, I was all on my own.

I was up early, dressed, and I went up on deck to get my purse and take my pill.

All was quiet; no one was stirring. At least I did not hear anything.

Suddenly Barry appeared. "Hello there, Rose, did you sleep well?" He asked.

I said, "Off and on, I am not used to sleeping on yachts; actually it's my first time. I was afraid I would have motion sickness and get sick, but so far so good. I was on a short dinner cruise once in Paris with Kedrick, other than that, this is my first time," and I tried to sound as normal as possible. I was petrified underneath my calm exterior; hopefully, none of it was showing.

"Good!" he said. "Let's have some coffee and cake, and I'll have you back in time for lunch with Kedrick."

"Did you hear any strange noises during the night?" he asked.

He went on to say that sometimes the sea makes strange ones, and it can be scary in the middle of the night particularly if you are not used to them.

"No! It was very still and peaceful," I answered.

"Where is Ruth?" I asked.

"Sleeping in, I guess; let me go get her," and he went to call Ruth, and I wondered if he knew I had seen him last night.

I said to myself, *Act normal, and see if you can find out as much as possible about him.*

I put the coffeepot on, and found a coffeecake in the refrigerator; yes, this yacht had everything, even gold fittings in the bathrooms—it was just like a floating hotel.

This much cost him a lot of money to keep. Was he that wealthy?

Ruth appeared looking the worse for the wear, hung over. Yes, she had quite a few glasses of wine last night.

I said, "Good morning, Ruth—did you sleep well?"

"I went straight to bed after you, and I don't remember anything until Barry called me this morning," she said.

"I have the coffee made, but I'm not a great coffee maker, so I hope it's okay; shall I pour you a mug?" I asked.

Barry appeared and said, "I smell the coffee."

We sat down, and I started asking the questions this time.

"How long have you known Kedrick?" I asked Barry.

"We went to school together, back in Rhodesia, and then I lost touch for years until I saw his name on a list of golfers about four years ago. I looked him up, and found out he was living here too, so I contacted him, and we get together as often as possible since. We were real good childhood friends.

"I travel with him sometimes, usually about twice a year, to London and Cairo mostly, and I have even caddied for him once, that was fun," he said.

He took a sip of his coffee, and went on to say, "The last few years have been rough for him, but I guess he has told you all about that. He deserves the very best, as he is a real genuine person, Rose. You couldn't meet a nicer person than Kedrick."

Well, this is more or less what Kedrick had told me.

Then I asked Ruth, "What do you do?"

"Oh! I run a jewelry store downtown, in the diamond district," she replied.

"That must be interesting, and you must meet all kinds of people there, wealthy I suppose to be able to afford such luxuries—any celebrities?" I asked.

"They usually have the items sent to their homes, so I really don't see them in person, only occasionally do I meet one," she replied.

"How long have you two known each other?" I asked both of them together.

Barry answered, "About four years. We are real good friends, right?" he said, and looked at her. "Yep, we are real good friends," she said.

We continued with small talk, and he said that we should be docking in about two hours, so enjoy the coastline, and take in whatever sun there is.

I sat up front, letting the gentle breeze blow through my hair, and wondered, *What have I learned?*

Nothing really! He had met Ruth four years ago and had looked up Kedrick four years ago.

Am I reading something into this or is it merely a coincidence? I asked myself.

Should I tell Kedrick or should I just keep quiet until I get back home, and perhaps then tell him in one of our phone conversations. I only had one more day here of what was the best holiday/vacation of my life, so I was really in a very confused state as to what to do next, and I was very scared.

I remembered something my nana had said to me once.

To keep out of trouble, just hear, see, and say nothing, so I decided to take her advice, and I hoped she was still praying for me. Wait until I tell her about my trip when I get back.

I was so looking forward to meeting up with Kedrick, so I put it at the back of my mind for now.

Barry had mentioned something about "Table Bay" and "Green Point" as points of interest (those names did not mean anything to me), and that we were heading back to dock. Time passed quickly.

I collected my bag and was ready to disembark, when I saw Kedrick strolling down the pier.

I called out to him, and he waved and quickened his pace towards us.

He came onboard and gave me a big hug and kiss, and I said, "Is everything all right?"

"Yes Rose, and I'll fill you in later," he said.

We chatted with Barry and Ruth for a few minutes; they were planning to stay onboard for the rest of the weekend.

I thanked them for their hospitality, and Kedrick and I left to go back to the hotel.

He carried my bag and held my hand as we walked along the pier. I just wanted to get back to the room and relax.

The past twelve hours had been very stressful, and I was scared.

We got to my room, and I just flopped down on the bed, and he came and lay beside me.

"I missed you," he said.

"Did your sister's visit at this time come as a big surprise?" I asked.

"Yes, it did," and he started to tell me the story.

"She had been asked at the last minute to accompany a patient on the air ambulance to a hospital here, and to take another patient back with them this morning. She did not have time to call me beforehand. I had given her the hotel phone number last week and told her I was here with you, and that's where she could find me if she needed to contact me.

"She said she would have loved to have been able to meet you; perhaps next time it can be arranged.

"She had to leave at 7:30 a.m. this morning, so she stayed over at the hospital last night.

"Hannah was thrilled to see her; we do not get to do that very often as she is preoccupied with her studies; she is doing her finals in a few months. We do talk at least once a week. She confided in me that she hoped to be engaged to her boyfriend soon. I have met him, and he is a real genuine person. He is studying to be a doctor too.

"I have told her about 'My Perfect Rose,'" and he leaned over and planted a kiss on my cheek.

"What would you like to do this afternoon?" he said as he reached for my hand. "I have booked a table for dinner at 8:00 p.m. at my favorite restaurant, so we are free until then."

"Can we just stay here by the pool and reminisce over the things we did this past two weeks? I go home tomorrow morning, you know," and I gave him a hug.

"I am well aware you leave in the morning," he said, "and we need to check my schedule to see when we can meet again."

He got up and went to his overnight bag, and took out his diary.

I noticed he never carried anything on him personally; even his wallet was in that little bag.

"Okay! Let's see…we are in April." He continued to check his diary and then said, "May, I play in Mauritius; June in Swaziland; July, I will be in Cairo; August is in Zaire and Mozambique (two tournaments actually), and September, I am in Toulouse in France."

I told him that I would never get off to go to any of those as I have no vacation left, but maybe I could manage a weekend in Toulouse, France.

"That means I won't get to see you for nearly five months," he said.

"We will just have to talk a lot on the phone in between and they say absence makes the heart grow fonder," and we both laughed.

We went down to sit by the pool; he got two spritzers, and I asked him how well he knew Barry and Ruth.

He told me he had lost track of Barry after school, but had run into him at a golf tournament here about four years ago, and he found out that they actually lived near each other.

"We see each other regularly now. I think I told you he comes to tournaments with me sometimes, usually mixes business with pleasure, as for Ruth, I have only met her a few times.

"I do not even know what she does or if, indeed, they are a pair. He acts weird at times, but then he was always a bit strange. I put it down to him being an only child, and losing his parents so young. Aunts raised him, and they too have died... Why so curious?" he asked.

"No reason," I said, "just me being inquisitive as usual."

We had a light lunch poolside and just chatted with other guests.

We found a very nice couple from Bath, England, on vacation here. We spent some time with them, and he was able to tell them about places to visit on their trip.

At around 5:00 p.m., we went back to the room to shower and change.

"We have about a thirty-minute drive to the restaurant," he said, "so we have plenty of time."

We showered together, and just held each other so close, and then dried each other off and got dressed. I wore the blue dress, as it was my last night, so I had kept this dress for this special dinner date.

I felt very good and he said, "I love you in blue; actually I love you in any color, and I just love to hold your hand."

We had a very romantic dinner in a quaint restaurant, and the food and wine were superb.

We got back to the hotel around 11:00 p.m. and went straight to bed.

We kissed, cuddled, made love, and fell asleep in each other's arms.

We both awoke around 7:00 a.m., and we made love again. We just lay there for a long time, neither of us saying anything.

Finally, I made a move to get up and he said, "Just ten minutes more in your arms," so I just lay back down.

When we did get up, we both showered, and I changed into my travel slacks and comfortable shoes and we headed down for breakfast.

My flight was for 12:30 p.m., so I was supposed to check in by 10:30 a.m.

Kedrick was driving me to the airport in his BMW car.

When we got to the airport, he said, "I will park first and go in with you and wait until your flight takes off." He took my case and carryon, and we went straight to the check-in desk.

Once I got my luggage checked in and got my boarding pass, we browsed around the airport shops, and I picked up a few souvenirs for my sisters and brothers.

I had bought Dad a pipe and Mam a silk scarf earlier. They were all small items, so I was able to put them in my carryon bag.

All too soon, it was time for me to board, and he just held on to me for ages.

I did not want to go, and he did not want me to go. I sensed this as he held me.

"We will talk each week until I see you in Toulouse in September," I said, as I kissed him goodbye.

"This has been the best holiday/vacation of my life," I told him.

"Mine too," he said and he kissed me again.

"We will have many more like this," he said, and then, "I have to go."

I looked back several times, and he looked so alone and lonely. My eyes were all teary the entire flight home, and my thoughts were racing. *Would I see him again? What about my fears? Was he involved in something with Barry?* I was very confused.

Barry and his strange actions had me troubled, and I tried so hard to erase them from my mind.

I wanted Kedrick so badly that I was not prepared to let anything come between us. I was in love.

WORK

The weeks went by; he called me several times each week, and we spent at least an hour on the phone. (It must be costing him a fortune, I kept thinking to myself.)

May went by, and then June, and then July, and this job of mine was getting boring, very boring. I really must seriously start looking around, and I started looking in the Sunday paper's employment supplement. It's time I made that move.

I went home for my mother's roast once a month, and updated Nana on my life.

She was failing very fast, and my grandfather was really out of it all together. It was really only a matter of time.

Dad and I had long walks and talks, and he was concerned about this long-distance relationship but said, "Rose, I am with you in whatever it is you decide to do."

This made me feel comfortable. I did not mention anything to him about what I had seen on Barry's yacht. We talked mostly about Nana and my grandfather James, and how ill they both were. "It's all in God's hands now," he said.

It was just past midnight when my father called to say my grandfather James had passed away. Funeral arrangements had already been planned, so I told him I would be there first thing in the morning. I had advised them at work that his death was imminent, so they knew I would be out for a few days.

Nana was much too weak to attend any of the services, so Cathay stayed with her.

As we left the churchyard following the burial, Cathay came rushing in, saying Nana had passed away. "She just lay down and closed her eyes. I heard a moan, and when I went to check on her, I could not find a pulse, so I called Doctor Carey, and he came and said, 'She's gone.'" She was so out of breath as she told us the story. While it came as a shock, we were not surprised.

Somehow, I just knew she could not live without him, I thought this to myself.

It was probably one of the worst days of my life. I questioned if there really was a God. I had lost both grandfathers and now Nana, all within a year.

I felt a big void in my life. I started to pray that Kedrick would help fill this void.

It was the second week in August when Kedrick called to say Hannah had passed away.

I said, "You have an angel in heaven," and I told him I would always keep her in my prayers.

I did not tell him about my grandparents' deaths. It was not the right time. He had his own sorrows to deal with right now. I would tell him next time I spoke to him. Now was not the time.

We talked for a little while and he said, "I may not get to call you again for a week or so, so don't get alarmed." I said that I fully understood, and to take all the time he needed, and to call me when he thought the time was right.

"I will still be in Toulouse in September, and I will send you your ticket before then; it's not for another five weeks," he said.

I said, "Don't worry, we will talk before then."

He said, "I need you, Rose, always remember that, and I do love you very much."

"I love you too, and I will be waiting for your call," I said, as we hung up.

I felt so sad for him. I wish I were there to comfort him, as he loved Hannah so much, but her suffering was over, and she is safe now in God's arms, and with his parents.

I very nearly booked a flight to go to him, but then realized that it was not the correct thing to do, so I just said a prayer for him and hoped that he had the strength to get through this terrible tragedy.

Work was now getting to me, and I said after September, I would get serious about job hunting.

I had my résumé made up, all ready to go.

I had known Kedrick fourteen months now, and each time we were together it's as if we had known each other all our lives, but I really did not know what the future held for us, and I still had that nagging question about Barry and his fake golf balls, and also if Kedrick knew about it. I did not have the courage to ask him about it; I was probably afraid of what he might answer, but then again, I just could not see him doing anything illegal or outside the law.

It was three weeks before I heard from him again. He sounded tired, and I asked him if he was okay. "I'm getting there," he said, "but it has been real hard—a lot harder than I expected. Considering she was sick for so long, it still came as a shock when it happened," and he gave a big sigh, and he was silent for a few seconds.

"Are you still on for the September trip?" he asked.

"Sure," I replied, "but only if you feel up to it though."

I went on to tell him about my grandparents' deaths, and he was so sympathetic, and he went on to say, "It's probably what we both need right now to get our minds off things. Have you any suggestions on what to do there?" he asked.

"I plan to take an extra vacation day on Friday, and take an early flight, so I should get there around 11:00 a.m.—is that too early for you?" I said.

"No, I will try to get there before you, or if not, I will travel late the night before and be there to meet you," he said.

"I will have to leave on Sunday evening as I have to be at work Monday morning, and you will have some time to yourself, and perhaps get in some practice rounds," I said.

"Rose, darling, it would be nice if you could stay longer, but I understand and I would love to visit the medieval city of Carcassonne on Saturday, and perhaps stay there for a night, if that's all right with you," he said.

"Kedrick, I would love that, as I have read someplace it's worth visiting, and I cannot wait for the next few weeks to go by," I said.

"Me neither, I will send you your ticket this week, but first, make sure you can get Friday off," he said.

We talked for another few minutes and then said, "Goodnight" and "I love you" to each other.

I went to HR and told them I needed an extra vacation day on Friday, the third one in September. Again, they made an issue out of it, and that alone convinced me I was to start looking for another job as soon as I got back.

Kedrick called to see if I had cleared the Friday and I said, "Yes."

"Okay, I will go ahead with the bookings then," he said.

We talked for at least another thirty minutes before we said, "Goodnight."

I could not wait for the third Friday in September to come around, and it was going to be my birthday in a few weeks. *I wonder if he will remember.* I asked myself.

TOULOUSE

I flew into Toulouse at 10:50 a.m. and just had a carryon bag, so I came straight out to see him standing there. We said nothing, just held on to each other for what seemed like hours; it really was just a few minutes. I thought he looked tired, but then again he had just been through a nightmare; losing Hannah must have been awful.

He took my bag, and we headed out to the car park where he had parked his rental car.

We sat inside, and he leaned over and gave me a big kiss, saying, "Rose, darling, it's so good to see you."

I just held him; we did not need words to express how we felt.

We spent three wonderful days in the South of France, and we did get to Carcassonne and stayed overnight there. It was everything and more that I expected it to be. I just wish Nana were alive for me to tell her all about it.

On the Saturday night after dinner in Carcassonne, he said, "I won't see you before your birthday, so I got a little something for you," and he handed me a little box.

Inside was a pin; it was a ladybug, with an emerald stone surrounded by diamonds.

It was just gorgeous. I do remember telling him in Granada that I liked ladybugs.

On Sunday, as we drove back to Toulouse, he mentioned his wife Sue, and that he was asking her to finalize the divorce papers as soon as he got back.

He understood she was seeing someone else, so there should not be any delay.

"All the paperwork has already been worked out since before Hannah got sick, so I do not expect any delay, and I understand she is ready to move on too."

I said nothing; I just listened.

"I am taking a few months off golf to get my affairs in order, but I would love if we could meet up for my birthday on December 19th in Paris, same hotel as before. You liked it there, so I will meet you in Paris on the 19th then, right?" he said.

I knew exactly what I would do. I would resign my job end of November, and take all of December off, and go job-hunting in January. (I did not tell him this just yet that those were my plans.) I would tell Kedrick all this in Paris. I wanted to wait until I had everything settled.

I said, "I will arrange the time off, and I can't wait to go back there again.

"Would you like to come back to Ireland with me for Christmas and meet my family? They are dying to meet you." I asked him.

"Yes! I think it's time I met your family, and I would love to spend Christmas with you in Ireland," he said.

We stopped just outside Toulouse and had a late lunch, early dinner, before he was to take me to the airport.

At the airport, we had coffee and just held hands. I had a weird feeling, but I guess it was just nerves, and I was wondering how my parents would react to his coming for Christmas. I am sure it will be fine. His divorce should be final by then, so this would not be an issue if it arose during the Christmas conversations. I had not told anyone he was married when I met him. Well, he was separated, and only Hannah's condition had him postpone the divorce.

It was time for me to board, and he hugged and kissed me and said, "I'm a lucky man to have found you." I just did not want to let him go.

I said, "I love you, and I will be looking forward to your phone calls."

I went through the boarding gate, and I watched as he waved through the glass door before he turned to go.

"I am the lucky girl," I said to myself.

He called me on my birthday on October 9th and said that he was signing the final divorce papers two days later. His sister had called him to say she had passed all her exams and was starting her residency, but she needed a favor from him. She told him she had also gotten engaged to her boyfriend.

She had organized a golf tournament for Leukemia Research Funds, and one of the golfers had to pull out, and wanted to know if there was any chance he would come up to Johannesburg and play, and also if he could get some other golfers as well to make the field interesting. It was scheduled for the last Sunday in October.

"Rose, I couldn't refuse her. I rounded up some English friends, and we are going there by private plane for the weekend. I probably won't get to call you that weekend, but I will call you before I go as it's nearly three weeks away."

He called twice again before his trip to Johannesburg and kept saying, "I can't wait to see you in Paris on the 19th of December." He told me he would arrange the tickets and hotel when he got back. "I will call you as soon as I get back from my trip to finalize the dates," he said.

He also told me that his divorce had been finalized, and all went very well. He was now a free man.

"I love you, my perfect Rose, and I will meet you in Paris," and we said goodnight.

I fell asleep that night thinking of his words to me— "I will meet you in Paris."

I just could not wait for that date to come. I could not wait to hold him again, and he was now a free man. I could boast about him to my friends and family. I had nothing to be ashamed about now.

I went to visit my parents that weekend and told them, and Dad said they were delighted to be finally meeting "the man." Mam was all excited; she had just received a letter from her cousin in Boston, and so with Kedrick's pending visit and the letter from cousin Sally in Boston saying that she too was coming to visit, she was in a real tizzy. "I am going to have the spare rooms painted to spruce them up." She said. "There she goes again," said Dad, "always ready with the paintbrush."

Cousin Sally was also bringing her older sister Betty with her. This was their first visit in twenty years, and they were both up there in years now. They were on my grandfather James' side of the family. His older sister had immigrated to Boston when he was just a child. He had never seen her since that day. Those were her children.

"When are they coming?" I asked her.

"No exact date yet, they are waiting for me to reply to say it is okay." She replied.

"Well, let me know, and I can take them to Dublin to show them the sights; that's if they are up to it," I said. It seems since President Kennedy came to Ireland to research his roots, Americans of all ages were tracing their roots in Ireland.

I also told them I was taking the month of December off, as I was considering selling my house and moving into the city center, perhaps just rent a condominium for a few months to see if I'd like it, before I purchased something else. I was also changing my job, something more interesting; I was bored in my present one.

I will do this in December while I am off, so "Dad, if I find something I like, will you come check it out for me?" I asked him.

"Sure! No problem," he said.

WAS IT TELEPATHY?

I got back late on Sunday night. I had a few messages on my answering machine, noting that there was nothing that important—Tim "my on again, off again" musician friend, wondering why I hadn't contacted him in months; my friend Brenda, wanting to set up a date for lunch; my friend Pat, wanting to know if I'd go to a Rolling Stones concert with her the end of next month. I just went to bed, as it was too late to reply to any of them. I would do it in the morning, or tomorrow night after work, or during the week, whenever.

I would do it as I always returned my calls; my friends knew that about me.

I snuggled down in my bed, pulling my white lace trimmed sheet around me, and fell asleep.

Something awoke me about an hour later, and I sat up in bed, but all was silent.

It took me ages to get back to sleep; *something was wrong someplace,* I kept thinking.

I said, "There goes my telepathy again." I finally relaxed, and fell into a restless sleep.

I got up very early in the morning, and I had decided to hand in my notice this coming Friday, which would be one month's notice as required. I was going to tell my boss Norman of my intentions this morning.

I really felt it was time to move on. I knew he would be upset as he relied on me a lot, but he would soon get over it, and I will have a month to train my replacement.

I never talked to anyone in the office about my relationship with Kedrick.

I did not even tell them I was seeing someone for over a year. You see, he was still technically a married man, and respectable girls did not date married men. It would be a black dot on my reputation. Well, he was free now, so perhaps I would tell them after my trip to Paris.

Some thought that it was my musician friend I was seeing, but I kept them all guessing.

I think my boss Norman suspected, but he never mentioned anything.

I got to the office feeling very confident that what I was doing was the right thing, and I did have my parents' blessing.

I read the paper, nothing exciting there, and I waited for Norman, my boss, to appear.

He strolled in with his coffee in one hand and his newspaper in the other.

"Good morning, Rose," he said.

"As soon as you are settled, may I see you for a few minutes?" I asked.

"Sure! I'll call you when I am ready," he replied.

We all knew he did the usual thing every morning: drank his coffee and then took his newspaper to the executive loo for at least half an hour.

Exactly thirty-five minutes later, he stuck his head out of his office door and said, "You can come in now, Rose."

Now I had butterflies in my tummy. *Was I doing the right thing?*

He asked how my weekend was, and I told him I had visited my parents, and I had got in late last night.

"I have something to tell you," I said.

He laughed and said, "You are pregnant."

"No, no," I replied very quickly. "I am handing in my notice on Friday, and I'll be leaving the end of November."

"I'm shocked; this is so sudden—why?" he asked.

"I feel the time is right for me to move on. I have nowhere to go here; all my colleagues are young, and they will probably be around for a long time. I need a bigger challenge," I said.

"Well, have you something lined up?" he asked.

"No," I said, and I told him all about my plans to take December off, and sell my house, and move into the city, and take it from there.

"I will be very sorry to see you go, and if there is anything I can do for you, please let me know; you were one of my best employees, and I certainly will miss you a lot," he said.

"I will need a reference," I said.

"That will be a real pleasure, Rose, and I will have my secretary Martha type it up in the next few days," he said.

I thanked him for being such a considerate boss over the years, and I told him I would gladly train whomever he appoints to take my place.

Company policy was to replace from within whenever possible.

I went back to my desk, and set my mind on doing my job for the rest of the day.

I have done the right thing, I kept telling myself.

The day dragged, and when I got home, I really was not hungry, so I just had a salad for dinner. Something was bothering me, but I did not know what. I just felt on edge.

I felt something was wrong somewhere.

I was hoping Kedrick might call; he should be back from Johannesburg by now.

No phone call, so I went to bed around 11:00 p.m.

Again, I could not sleep, so I tossed and turned for hours. I just had this very uneasy feeling that something was wrong.

I was up very early, as I wanted to type my letter of resignation before anyone came into the office. I typed it, signed it, and said, "Heck! I will hand it in today, why wait until Friday."

They are so messed up in HR they probably will not get to it until Friday anyway, and it will take them the whole month to get my papers in order.

I slipped the envelope under the HR manager's door, and headed back to read the newspaper.

Nothing exciting caught my eye, so I went back over it again to see if I had missed anything (something I had never done before).

Then, I saw a small article on the sports page. I can still see it to this day.

It read: "Two British and three South African golfers, along with four other passengers and three crewmembers, are reported missing and presumed dead after their private plane crashed shortly after takeoff from Johannesburg Airport, en route to Cape Town. The golfers had been to Johannesburg for the weekend to play in a charity tournament for Leukemia Research. No further details are available at this time, and no names have been released."

I think I actually died for a few seconds then. My hands went numb, and I felt my head spinning, and then I must have passed out.

I came around, then I saw a few people around me, and I heard my assistant Kathy say, "She is coming around."

They had called an ambulance, and the medical team was there checking me out.

I said, "I just fainted. I'll be fine, please just take me home, Kathy."

The chief of the response team said, "Her vital signs are fine," and then he asked me if I would like to go to the hospital to be checked out completely, and "Did you have some kind of shock?" he asked.

I said, "I will call my own doctor when I get home," and I proceeded to gather my belongings, and the paper, and got ready for Kathy to drive me home.

Kathy drove me in my car, and another girl from the office came behind us to bring her back. They both came in with me and asked what had happened.

I said, "I had not been feeling well for the past two days, so I guess it's the flu."

They left and said I was to call them if I needed anything.

I called my friend Pat and asked her to drop by after work.

She asked if I was okay. "You sound awful. I'll come right over," she said.

I said, "No! I'll just lie down and you can come over after work."

I just wanted the house to myself, while I tried to pull myself together. I just lay on my couch for over an hour and thought, *This is not happening to me.*

I read the article in the paper, repeatedly.

I kept saying, "Please, God, he was not on that plane," and I prayed as I never prayed before that he was alive, and that he had missed that flight, or just stayed on with his sister for a few days, anything, just as long as he was alive.

I just sipped some water, and then I picked up the phone and called his number in Cape Town.

I got his answering machine, so I left a message for him to call me as soon as he got in.

I called every hour on the hour, until Pat arrived at 5:30 p.m.

I told Pat what happened, and I showed her the newspaper article. She just hugged me and said, "It's not definite that he was on that plane. Perhaps he missed that flight and was on another plane."

I just looked at her and said, "He was on that plane; he would have called me by now."

"Let me fix you something to eat, and then we will try the BBC radio and TV to see if there is any news about the accident on it—remember, British golfers were onboard too," she said.

I said, "I just can't eat now," and she snapped back, "You haven't eaten all day; you need your strength now above all times—and you have to be strong."

She made a plate of finger sandwiches, and I just picked and nibbled at some.

We kept the TV and the radio on to see if there was anything new about the plane crash, being a private plane, and being in South Africa, so far away, there wasn't much interest by the media, and communications were very limited. It was not a proper golf tournament, only a charity outing. I guess the media may not even have covered it.

The BBC nine o'clock news had a small report on it. It merely said what was in the newspaper article that morning, but it did name the two British golfers, nothing about the South African ones. I knew Kedrick was friends with both of those golfers, so my heart sank again.

I called his number again, and still the answering machine came on. I did not leave any more messages; I just hung up with a heavy heart.

Pat said, "I'll go home and pack a bag, and I will stay with you for a few nights."

"I appreciate that, and I will make up the spare bed for you," I said.

Pat was back within the hour, and we headed up to bed.

I asked her to call my office in the morning, and tell them I would be out for the whole week, "Tell them I have the flu," I said.

"Are you sure you don't want me to stay home with you tomorrow? I can take a vacation day or two," she said.

"I'll be fine during the day, and having you at night will be a great comfort," I told her.

I said "goodnight" to her and that I would see her in the morning, before she left for work.

I tried calling his number again, but still the same. I guess I just wanted to hear his voice on the answering machine.

I did not sleep at all; I saw every hour on the clock, and I kept thinking I could hear the phone ringing, but it was all in my imagination. I even thought I heard him calling my name.

Pat stayed until the weekend. I tried repeatedly calling his number, and each time it was just his answering machine.

The Saturday newspaper, an English one, did have another article on the crash. It was all about the British golfers, but did name the other passengers onboard that flight, and yes, his name was listed. However, it also said one caddie had survived, but was in a coma, and in serious condition, and his chances of survival were slim.

I just went numb all over. I remembered another of Nana's sayings: "Remember, life is just a memory; close your eyes and you can see."

I closed my eyes; I could see Kedrick holding out his hand to me, and then he vanished from sight.

I went back to work on Monday and just kept to myself. Norman my boss asked, "Are you feeling better?" and I said, "Yes, but I am still very weak. I guess I got a bad dose of the flu."

I now had only three weeks to put in at work, and I struggled with every day and every night.

I rang Kedrick's number every night, and after two weeks, the answering machine was full and it could not accept any more messages.

My friend Pat was the only one aware of the real reason I was feeling unwell, and she was supportive and she said, "Rose, changing jobs and house hunting is just the thing you need to take your mind off things; also, please do tell your family," she said.

I had to get my strength back, so she made an appointment with my doctor for me.

I found out later she had told him the full story, and he never let on.

He was so nice to me, and suggested a mild sedative for a month to help me get back on my feet. "That flu can really do a job on you. Come back in ten days and I will see how you are doing," he said.

MOVING ON

Norman, my boss, had arranged a farewell dinner for me on the last Friday of my working there, and during dinner, one of the staff mentioned the golf tournament. He said they were in the final stages of planning for the next one, and he turned to me and said, "Rose, you will be missed; you were great last time... by the way, did you ever hear from that good-looking golfer that took a real shine to you?"

I said, "No!"

I could not wait to get out of there, but I had to wait for a presentation.

I was given a presentation of some Waterford Crystal.

I cried all the way home, and all that night. *Is there a God? Why is he doing this to me?* I kept saying to myself. I prayed to Nana that she would see me through this nightmare.

I decided to go home for a week and tell Dad what had happened. I would tell him the full story of my relationship, and perhaps he would come back with me to get the house ready for the market.

Dad and I took long walks, and I told him the full story and how I felt.

He was so supportive and said, "It's better to have loved and lost than never loved at all; remember, Rose, you are still very young."

Dad came back with me for a week, and he drove his own car. He was back driving again, so he followed my car.

We got the house all ready for showing, and I decided to rent a condominium in the city for twelve months, until I decided where to go from there. I would also do temp work only for those twelve months, and when I finally got a permanent job, then I would buy another house as near to the job as possible.

The house was sold in two weeks. It was a very pretty house, but again, I felt I needed to move on; however, I would miss my rose gardens, and my waterfall.

That part of my life was now past tense.

I moved into the condominium, and the first thing I did was get a phone installed, I got my number ex-directory, as I felt I really needed to move on and make new friends.

My real friends, well I could always contact them with my new number.

I still rang Kedrick's number every week, and I got the same message, "Answering machine full."

Soon, the 19th of December arrived, and I went to my church that morning and said a prayer for him and Hannah. It was his birthday today, and we were to meet in Paris to celebrate.

How can God be so cruel?

It was not a good day. I just came home and cried all day long; actually, I cried myself to sleep.

I think this was the worst day of my life. This was even worse than the day my grandparents died.

I spent Christmas with my family, and I tried my best to get into the spirit of things, but my thoughts always went back to Kedrick. He should be here with us. He had promised me he would come to meet my family this Christmas.

I stayed there until after New Year's, and then headed back to my condominium in the city.

I felt it was time I got back to work.

I signed on with a temporary agency, and I was working the next day.

I was very lucky, and I usually got temporary jobs for six to ten weeks at a time.

It was now February, and I tried Kedrick's number again.

I just do not know why I kept calling; I could not accept that he was dead. My brain just would not accept it. I kept hearing his voice in my sleep.

This time, I finally got a message that sank in: *I had to accept that he was gone.* "The number you have dialed is no longer in service."

I dialed it twice; just to make sure this is what I heard.

My friends, by now, were all aware of what had happened, and they were always there for me, as was my family. If I needed to talk or go out to lunch or dinner, one or the other was always there.

It was as if they had a behind-the-scenes intervention to help me through.

Soon it was approaching the last Sunday in October, and I decided to go home to my family. I felt it would be too painful to be alone. I had also started having dreams that he was dancing with me, and we were listening to our song, "Strangers in the Night." I usually woke up in a sweat.

I got back to the city just after 7:00 p.m., and ran a bath, and I just relaxed in there for a long time.

I had just started another temporary job, and I was delighted to find that my new boss was someone I had worked with previously. We got on really well, and one day he asked me if I would be interested in a permanent position. I said, "I'll think about it."

It was probably time to find something permanent anyway.

The position offered to me was as a Financial Consultant in the airline industry.

I would have to travel overseas at least four to six times a year. I was to consult with all the big accounts and reconcile any discrepancies. The money and benefits were excellent, and it did involve travel.

I talked to my family and all my friends, and they all said, "Go for it, it's time you moved on."

I accepted the position, and I decided to start house hunting. The lease was up on the condominium anyway; I had been renewing it on a month-to-month basis.

I called Dad and asked him if he could come up for a weekend, and that my realtor Lisa would line up some homes for us to see. I told her exactly what I was looking for, and she found two homes that she thought I would like. Both were in great areas, and not too far from work. They were also near the water, and this was my dearest wish to be able to walk by the ocean. I loved the ocean; it had a calming effect on me.

I asked Dad's advice and he said, "Both are in good shape." I put in an offer for both properties, and whichever came first is the one I would buy. I liked both very much; they had the entire requirements I had asked for. They were actually on the same street. Each on opposite ends. It was a very pretty tree-lined street.

Soon, I was moving again. My new home had a beautiful rose garden; I think this was a key selling point for me anyway. I had another new phone number, and again, I had it ex-directory and I only gave it out to my close family and friends.

I had my new home completely redecorated to my taste, nice pastel shades, but it had color and warmth to it. My neighbor Ellie came over with a bottle of wine to welcome me to the neighborhood. Lovely lady in her mid to late eighties, I guessed.

I told her my mother's cousins from Boston were coming to visit; they had planned to come last year, but Betty took ill at the last minute, so they postponed their trip until now. I told her I would introduce her to them.

They arrived a month later, and Dad drove them up to my house.

I invited Ellie to join us all for dinner one evening, and it was probably the most enjoyable evening I had in a long time. You should hear some of their stories. It was just great. Dad and I showed them around and they left to go back two days later. It was a short visit, but very interesting. I had not seen them since I was a child. Well, it was over twenty years ago; a lot of water had run under the bridge since then. I told them I would certainly visit with them if I ever got to Boston.

My friends were now pushing me to start dating again and to start going out more.

I settled in to my new job, and my new home, and I had started to get on with my life, painful as it was. Yes! It still hurt a whole lot.

Kedrick was the love of my life, my soul mate, and he would always have a portion of my heart.

I found it very hard at first to date. I am sure I was very boring, but I did try.

I guess it was very unfair to the men I dated; I was always comparing them to Kedrick or vice versa.

TRUE FRIENDS

My girlfriends, Pat and Brenda, dropped by unannounced one Sunday afternoon.

I was just lying around taking it easy when the doorbell rang. I peeped out to see who was there, and I quickly went to the door to let them in.

"Surprise, surprise," they both shouted in unison. "We were just out for a drive and we decided to come by to help cheer you up," said Brenda.

"Great, let me put the kettle on for a cuppa," I said.

"I brought a bottle of nice wine," said Pat.

"Who is driving?" I asked.

"Brenda," replied Pat.

"Okay, it's tea for Brenda then," I said.

We went into the kitchen and I put the kettle on and took out two wine glasses and a bottle opener. I put the bottle of wine on ice for a few minutes while I prepared the tea for Brenda.

"We would like to talk to you about Kedrick," said Brenda.

"Nothing really to talk about," I replied.

"Oh, yes, there is," said Pat.

They both went on to say it was time I forgot all about him and moved on with my life, both taking turns with their comments.

Brenda said, "Rose, you really didn't get to know him that well—did you? From what you have told us, he never took you to see his home in Cape Town and he never introduced you to any of his friends other than that rich geek. Does that not seem strange to you?"

"You have to understand the circumstances," I told them.

Pat asked, "What circumstances?"

"Well, he was still legally married. I had kept my relationship with him pretty quiet too, only my family and you two knew the true story, so I assume he was doing the same thing," I replied.

"I don't see it that way," said Brenda, "actually I think he had his cake and ate it too."

"No, no, it's not a bit like that," I shouted back at her, "I know he took Hannah to his home, his condo by the water, and I assume he had to have a hospital bed and oxygen there, so he didn't want me to see that. He did say the time wasn't right and I trusted him and he did get divorced," I replied rather angrily.

"We are just trying to get you back living your life again," said Pat, and they both reached out and took my hands.

"I know, and I am very grateful for your concerns, but really, I will be just fine," I told them.

They both stayed quite late, and we really had a heart-to-heart talk about everything—life in general and the ups and downs of love and its demands.

I felt so much better afterwards.

I went to bed that night thinking to myself, *I knew my Kedrick and he was the real thing.*

I had never mentioned to anyone that I did have some questions about him—in particular, his relationship with Barry or, as Brenda put it, that rich geek. My mind was racing as I tried to get to sleep. Eventually, sleep did come, but I still had the same questions on my mind when I awoke.

Once again, I began to question if I would ever find closure. *Would I get the answers to all my questions?*

Time will tell, but one thing, no one can take away my memories of those Paris nights and those Cape Town days.

I will always have the memory of him holding my hand.

SEVEN YEARS LATER

Seven years later, I was still enjoying my job, and my home, and I kept up with the latest fashions. I had trips to Germany, Sweden, France, England, Belgium, and Denmark and of course several to the USA. I had also met up with my "on again, off again" musician friend Tim, and we started seeing each other whenever he was in town.

He had been married, but had divorced, and had two children from his marriage.

My mother's cousins from Boston, Sally and Betty, visited once more, but they were now very feeble, so we all knew it would be their last visit. I think they knew too.

Some of my friends tried to set me up with dates, and some I went on, but it was just to get out. I had no real interest.

One night in particular, one of the secretaries from work called to say her boyfriend was coming to town for the weekend, and he was bringing a friend with him, and would I like to have dinner with them to make up a foursome.

I said, "Sure," and I arranged to have her pick me up, and go straight to the restaurant.

We had a lovely meal, and it was suggested that we go dancing afterwards.

I loved to dance, so I said, "Sounds good to me."

My date was a real nice guy, and tall, dark, and handsome. He was not very talkative, but boy did he dance. We danced until the wee hours of the morning, and his friend said he would loan him his car for him to drive me home. He drove me home, and asked if he could come in for a coffee. I said it was too late and that he had to get the car back anyway.

He asked if he could call me next time he was in town, and I said, "Yes, that would be nice," and we kissed and said goodnight.

He called me at least once a month for about four months; we met and had dinner, and of course, we went dancing. I never asked him to stay over, and I was glad to have him as my dancing partner. I found out by accident that he was in a seminary, training to be a priest.

Well, that was the end of that, and I was very annoyed with the girl from work having set me up like that. She always maintained she did not know.

Another of my male friends turned out to be married. I knew he had been married, but he told me he was separated, and had no contact with his wife for years. I found out later he was still living with her, and they had one daughter. I really was not having any luck with men. I usually went back to my friend, Tim the musician.

I felt secure with Tim, as I had known him since I was seventeen. He lived up north in Belfast.

I also had met a very nice man from Sweden; Sven was his name, and we had dinner whenever he came to Ireland on business. I found out later he too was married, and I was just a diversion for him, but he remained a friend, even after we broke up.

His marriage was not a good one, and this time he was telling the truth.

I guess at my age, all the men either are married, or confirmed bachelors, or gay.

My friends, Pat and Brenda, came away with me for a week's vacation every year.

We went to Spain, Majorca, Greece, Canary Islands, Italy, and all the usual holiday spots over the years.

I was enjoying life, but my thoughts always went back to Cape Town, and what if he had lived— would we have ended up together?

I still had dreams about him, always very romantic ones.

I made a promise that someday I would go back, when the "pain had gone" (if it ever goes away). I would try to find out what happened, and see if I could locate Barry or Ruth, and perhaps find his grave. I had no one to contact over there. I did not have a phone number or address for Barry or Ruth, and I did not even know his or her last names.

While Kedrick often mentioned his sister, he never actually said her name, not that I can recall anyway. I remember him saying it was just the two of them.

A lot had happened in those seven years.

Space travel was common now; communications were much better, and we were now getting the news from around the world on a twenty-four-hour channel.

Travel was getting less expensive, and more and more people were traveling; the world was becoming a smaller place to live in.

I was put in charge of the social club at work. I was elected its chairperson, and this kept me busy. I had a function to arrange each month, like soccer games, tennis games, and children's parties at Christmas, but the big one was the Christmas Dinner Dance.

I never brought a partner with me to any of them, and all my friends told me to bring someone, as people were beginning to talk. Rumor had it I was ill or there was something wrong with me, so I decided to ask my friend Tim from now on, if he was available.

This worked out very well, and tongues stopped wagging.

I still visited my family at least once a month, and I noticed that both had more grey hairs and more lines each time I came home to visit with them. They were both in good health, and only my younger sister Violet was still living at home.

My other three siblings had moved out, and they were enjoying their careers. I laughed when Dad said, "Mam is still very handy with the paintbrush."

It was coming up to Christmas, and I had already done my Christmas shopping, when Tim called one night and said, "Rose, there is a big concert in London in February. It's a charity event and lots of artists will be there; would you like to come with me for the week?"

"I will have to check out my schedule at work to see if any trips have been scheduled for me that week, and I will get back to you," I said.

"Good, but I will need to know before the end of this week (it was Tuesday) as all the hotels are nearly booked up already, so we need to act fast," he said.

"I'll check it out in the morning when I get into the office and call you tomorrow night; will you be home?" I asked.

"Yes! I don't have a gig until Thursday," he replied.

He played drums, and he was a lovely singer. I loved his rendition of "Suspicious Minds," an Elvis number, one of my all-time favorites.

Next day, after checking my planner for February, I was delighted to see I had nothing scheduled, so I arranged to take that week off.

This event was to be a weeklong affair; they had rehearsals, and a program timetable had to be set up before the big day on Saturday.

I called Tim that night and told him, and he said his manager was taking care of all the travel plans, so he would ask him to include my name on the list. He would give me all the details later, once they were finalized, but "I will probably see you before then anyway," he said.

We talked a little longer about various things, and I said, "I am tired, and I need to get to bed. See you soon, Tim," and I hung up.

Christmas for me was still a very painful time. Kedrick's birthday was on the 19th.

I still went to church on the last Sunday in October, and on his birthday, and I said a prayer for him and Hannah. I never missed a year, and my friends kept telling me to let go. I also visited Nana's grave and asked her help.

After all those years, I still was not accepting his death. I needed that trip to Cape Town. I needed closure. Deep down, I felt he was still alive out there somewhere, but where? I was still not accepting his death. I had no proof.

Christmas came and went, and I began to prepare for a trip to New York in January.

I had been there over a dozen times now, always on business trips, and I had always enjoyed it. I had also made some friends, and they usually put out "The Red Carpet" for me when I arrived.

They took me to Broadway shows, ball games, and even a golf tournament.

I had never watched or read the results of any golf tournaments since Kedrick's plane crash, so I was a little apprehensive about going, but once I got there I was okay, but I was very glad when it was over. It brought back so many emotions. I did not recognize any of the names; it was just a local charity event.

I always went on a shopping spree when in New York, and I picked up some nice pieces of clothing, but for some reason, they did not last very long.

A friend once said, "It's a throwaway society over there, all quantity, no quality," and you know, I am beginning to think he is right, at least in some cases anyway.

However, I enjoyed them while they lasted.

I met one male friend on one of my first trips to New York. We met at a function, and friends introduced us. Every time I came back to New York, we made sure we kept an evening free for dinner. He was English, and his name was Piers Somersby, I guess about forty or so, and he traveled a lot, he was an art dealer.

He was the typical bachelor, and he never intended to settle down.

He enjoyed having a pretty woman on his arm when he went out, but for some reason, we felt so comfortable together, and we were able to pour our hearts out over dinner. It was always a real treat having dinner with him.

It was not a romantic relationship, more like brother, sister, and for me, that suited me fine.

He very rarely visited Ireland, but he said he would try to get there someday soon, and I could show him around. It had been more than ten years since he last visited there. "I have heard lots of things have changed over the years," he said. "Some for the better and some not too good."

I said, "Don't believe all you read in the papers, and even half of all you see on TV. The media gets it wrong, sometimes very wrong."

He became a real good friend to me, and again, I remember my nana's quotes: "Good friends are like angels; you don't have to see them to know they are there."

It was a very successful trip, businesswise, and I even got a large bonus when I got back. I did not have any time to visit with my cousins on this trip either. I never get the time to go visit with them; all my days are planned out for me. I will tag on a few days' vacation soon, and visit with them all. They keep asking why I do not make time to visit; I am not sure they understand what a business trip entails.

I had found large discrepancies in an account, all to our advantage.

Their accounting practices were somewhat different from ours. Sometimes two sets of books, I noticed.

Soon it was time to pack my bags for London, my trip with Tim.

I had family over there, and while Tim was rehearsing, I would visit with them.

My thoughts went back to my last visit to London with Kedrick. He had promised me we would come back. It hurt—it hurt a lot, but in fairness to Tim, I tried to put the past behind me, for now anyway.

CHARITY CONCERT LONDON

Tim flew from Belfast; I flew from Dublin, and we met up at the hotel.

We had a lovely time, and I caught up with all my cousins, and what they were doing.

My! How time flies, the years were passing by very quickly. Last time I saw them, the children were small, now they are teenagers, and all grown up.

I was to spend all day Friday with Tim; they had a rest day before the concert.

We took in all the sights, and when passing Chelsea Registry Office, he suddenly grabbed hold of me, and said in a very serious voice, "Rose, let's get married."

This took me by surprise. I guess I had known Tim so long, and I suppose I did love him in some form, but marriage never entered my head.

He was Belfast Protestant and divorced, and I was Irish Catholic.

All the troubles up North were all about this, Protestant v. Catholic, and it would never work.

I looked at him and said, "Why spoil a perfect relationship by getting married," and we both laughed, and we went on with our sightseeing tour.

The concert on Saturday was a big success, and buckets of money was collected for the various charities.

I flew back to Dublin; he flew back to Belfast, and no mention of his marriage proposal was ever mentioned again by either of us.

MY HIGH-SCHOOL CRUSH

It was during one of my many visits home that I ran into an old school friend of mine. Actually, I had a real crush on him at school.

Billy and I were very close, and we dated off and on for nearly two years, but we decided to go our separate ways.

We remained very good friends through the years and then someone told me he had immigrated to Australia. It was more than ten years since I had seen him, and it was quite by accident that I had run into him again.

Yes, I literally bumped his car while parking. Thankfully, no damage was done, and he invited me out for a coffee; he knew I did not drink when I was driving.

We talked over old times, and we got caught up on our lives since we last met. He had gone to medical nursing school and became a nurse practitioner after college. My friends from school had told me some time ago that he had gotten into some kind of trouble and had gone to Australia. It appears he had given the wrong medication to a patient, but thankfully, it was discovered before any damage was done to the individual. He was dismissed from his job and then he decided to immigrate for a few years, until the story faded from memory and hopefully he could come back someday, and work as a nurse again.

Well, he was back, and I discovered he was working in a nursing home in Dublin.

I told him to drop in and see me sometime, and I gave him my address and phone number. I always liked Billy, but again, it was as a friend, nothing more.

I did not let on that I knew anything about his dismissal, and he never mentioned it to me either. He told me he had married an Australian girl, but she had drowned in the swimming pool six months later. She had some kind of seizure, and the autopsy could not determine the exact cause of her death. She had been on the birth pill, and had been suffering from some kind of tummy bug, but it was thought to be just some kind of flu bug.

He went on to tell me that he was devastated, as he really loved her very much, and he could never settle with anyone else since then. (Oh! How I know that feeling.)

"How long ago did this happen?" I asked him.

"Two years," he replied.

"Billy, time is a great healer," I told him.

"Liar, liar, Rose," I said under my breath. It was like déjà vu all over again.

Somehow, I did not feel I should tell him my story; something held me back.

It was still very painful to talk about it. Billy did call me about two weeks later, and we arranged to meet for dinner. I enjoyed our night out, and said, "We must do this more often." "Yes, we definitely should," he said.

He kissed me on the cheek, as I sat inside my car to drive home.

On my way home, I kept thinking it was nice to know I had another friend I could call if I needed to talk. Yes, it was Tim and Billy who seemed to be the most stable individuals in my life now. I had a romantic on-again, off-again relationship with Tim and a platonic one, for now, with Billy.

I saw Billy several times over the next few months, and I noticed he seemed to have a lot of money. He drove a very expensive top of the range car, wore designer clothes, and he seemed to have several watches, gold rings, and gold chains, all very expensive jewelry of good quality. I knew my jewelry. I wondered how he could afford all this on a nurse's salary.

I decided to do a little snooping to see if I could find out anything more about him. Did he have a secret life I did not know about? He had never suggested we get romantic, and this suited me, and yes, I did enjoy his company.

He was witty, charming, and a real gentleman. Well, he was to me anyway.

One thing bothered me; he never told me where he lived. I had asked him once, and his reply was,

"Here and there, I have a room at the nursing home too."

I looked at him and said, "So you have no permanent address?"

"I'm looking for the right place," he replied.

I guess he had just come back from Australia a few months prior, and he was taking his time in finding the right place. It seemed a perfectly good and sensible idea, yes, and a very sensible thing, not rushing into anything.

I was still very curious, so I called a few of my old school friends to see if they knew he was back. None of them seemed to know anything about him; they too had not seen him for over ten years. We all came to the same conclusion that he was a very elusive person for the past ten years.

I told them what he had told me about his life and his wife, and how devastating it had been for him. One friend Judy seemed very surprised about this. "I never thought he would marry. I always suspected he was gay. Well, who knows?" she said.

This comment set me thinking. Could it be true? Was I just his experiment in school? Maybe that is why our relationship never amounted to anything.

I sure did pick them I did—didn't I?

I put it out of my mind and decided to continue seeing him, as he made no sexual demands on me. Therefore, what if he was gay, if he was, he was.

This news did not bother me at all; he is still Billy, and my friend.

Months went by and I never did tell Billy about Kedrick. I felt uneasy about telling him.

He often asked why I never married, and I always replied, "I am waiting for my knight in shining armor to come sweep me off my feet, yes, I am waiting for Mr. Right."

I suspect my reasoning for not telling him is he has had enough tragedy in his life, so I did not want to burden him with mine.

One day, a day I will always remember, I received a letter at my office.

The mail boy handed it to me and said, "Rose, you must have an admirer."

I did not recognize the writing; it was all in caps anyway, and both my name and address were printed. "Who on earth would be writing to me at my office?"

I slid open the envelope and took out just a one-page note, all printed.

It read:

"IF YOU VALUE YOUR LIFE, YOU MUST STAY AWAY FROM BILLY. BE WARNED."

I started to shake, and one of the girls asked if something was wrong. I never answered her. I just got up from my desk and went straight to my boss's office. I showed him the letter; he asked me who Billy was, and I told him the whole story. He picked up the phone and called the police. "Rose, keep the envelope too," he said.

The police questioned me, and they sent someone to question Billy at his workplace. That was the only place I knew where he could be found.

I only had phone contacts for him, no address.

I got home, called Pat, told her the story, and she said, "Just let the police handle it, Rose."

Next day, the police were back to take fingerprints from all the staff, including mine. They had found prints on the note, and they had to exclude mine as I had handled it. My boss had to be excluded also; he had handled it when I gave it to him to read. They found no match at my office, and they informed me that the prints were not a match for Billy either.

The interesting thing was Billy never contacted me, no phone call—nothing.

I tried calling him several times, but the phone just rang and rang, no one picked up. I still did not know exactly where he lived, but he had given me two phone numbers where I could contact him. He kept telling me he still had not found the right place yet.

The police inspector, a nice man called Mr. Looney, said he would keep me in the picture as to any new developments.

A week went by, and of course, Pat and Brenda kept calling to see if I had any news, and I told them I was still in the dark as to what was going on.

"You do pick them," said Pat.

Billy finally called one week later, and we arranged to meet for dinner, next night, which was Friday. He always took me to very upscale restaurants, and this time it was no different.

I tried to ask him what was going on, but he said, "Just wait until I see you."

We were both silent for a while and then he said, "Rose, I apologize for all the stress I have caused you."

I just looked at him and said, "Enlighten me please, what is going on?"

He just stared at me. "Do you know who sent me that threatening letter?"

He hesitated for a second and then said, "Oh Rose, it's a very long story," he said.

"Well Billy, I have plenty of time, so let me hear all about it."

I tried to remain calm as we proceeded to order, and I waited for him to continue his story. "When I was in nursing school, I became very friendly with another male nurse. Rose, back then I was very confused as to my sexuality; I thought I might be bisexual. He became very possessive, and he was always following me and harassing me. I tried to finish with him several times, and that is when I decided to go to Australia. It wasn't my job loss; you know about that, I assume, the medicines' mix-up and all that? That's not the reason I decided to go; it was my stalker friend, which was the real reason I left."

I pretended not to know what he was talking about. "What job loss and medicine mix-up?" I asked him.

"Rose, I thought everyone knew about that," he replied.

"No, tell me, Billy," I said.

"Well, one night while I was on duty, he came into my ward and tried to cause a scene. I tried to calm him down, and I took him to the pill cabinet to get him something to calm his nerves, as he was very uptight. In hindsight, I should just have called the police.

"I had my tray all ready to give out my patients' medicine, and I left it down while I got him some Valium. He calmed down eventually and went home.

"To this day, I think he was the one that switched the medicine on my tray. Remember, he was a nurse too, so he knew what he was doing.

"I suspect he was trying to set me up, hoping perhaps, I would just come running back to him.

"Well, I took the blame, and I was fired and I went to Australia. I thought I had gotten rid of him. I found a job as a private nurse, and I made good money, and my life seemed to be settling down.

"Then a wonderful thing happened to me; I fell in love with this beautiful woman and we got married. I really did love my wife; our wedding picture was in the local papers, and everyone said we were the perfect couple. It seems a friend of his who lived in Australia saw it, and mailed it to him.

"This friend seemed to know who I was and that he had been looking for me.

"He came to Australia and eventually tracked me down through the photographer that took our wedding pictures.

"He arrived on our doorstep one evening, and my wife answered the door.

"He told her he was a good friend of mine, and she invited him in.

"I was out on the patio by the pool, and I nearly fainted when I saw him.

"He had this evil grin on his face. I just knew he was going to be trouble—big trouble.

"He told us he had found a job at the local hospital, and he had an apartment nearby. Lucky for me, it was not the hospital where I now worked. I was head nurse practitioner there now. Well, to cut a long story short, he started to blackmail me.

"It went on for five months, and each time he wanted more and more money.

"I had to tell my wife, and she was supportive, and we decided we would go to the police.

"I can recall during one of his visits to our house, my wife was talking about insurance, and she told him we had both taken out very large life policies on each other after we married. 'Just in case,' she had said this in a laughing way.

"Then the nightmare started; my wife was found dead in our pool, before we got to the police. I was investigated and eventually cleared of any wrongdoing.

"He vanished, and again to this day, I think he may have had something to do with her death, but I had no proof.

"I inherited a lot of money from my wife's estate, and a year later, I came back home thinking the nightmare was finally over, and I could start a new life.

"Then this letter was sent to you. I could not believe it—not again.

"I told the police the full story, and they told me not to contact you for a few days.

"I guess they had to check my background to see if I was telling them the truth.

"I think this Inspector Looney has a soft spot for you. I went looking for this guy.

"It was not too hard as I had access to the nurses' association, and with Inspector Looney's help, we tracked him down. They are keeping track of his movements, and they hope to have a search warrant in place tomorrow to obtain his fingerprints, and search his home.

"Rose, I am so sorry to get you mixed up in something like this.

"You are one of my best friends, and I love and respect you very much."

I reached over, touched his hand, and said, "Billy, I am here for you if you ever want to talk. I consider you my best friend too, and I hope they put this guy away for life."

We finished the rest of our meal and then Billy said, "Now you know why I move a lot," he sighed and went on to say, "I was always afraid he would come after me again for money; he knows I inherited a lot."

"Billy, Inspector Looney will take care of everything; it's going to be all right." I said.

I kissed him on the cheek as we said goodnight, and I drove home, scared, but relieved Billy had brought everything out in the open.

Next morning, just after seven a.m., my phone rang. "Who the heck is calling me so early on a Saturday morning?" I shouted aloud. Usually it can be bad news this early in the morning. "I just hope it's not Mam or Dad," I said to myself as I picked up the phone. "Rose, it's Inspector Looney, and I have bad news for you."

"What is it?" I shouted back to him. I was actually screaming, and I did not realize it.

"It's Billy; he was shot last night, and we have a suspect in custody."

"How bad is it?"

"I'm sorry, Rose; he is dead."

"Oh my God," and I screamed it repeatedly.

"I am on my way over to see you, and I will fill you in on what's been happening in the case. I will explain everything to you; in the meantime, stay calm."

It was a Saturday morning and all my nightmares started to come back to me. "Was I bad luck to all my men friends?" I asked myself.

I called Pat and told her, and she said she would come over straight away.

Inspector Looney arrived and told me the whole story.

"It appears Billy was followed from the restaurant where you dined last night.

"This stalker friend of his was watching you both eat. We were trailing him but unexpectedly he pulled alongside Billy's car and shot him in the head.

"It came as a shock; we never expected this to happen. Billy was dead on arrival at the hospital. We arrested the shooter, and you should see what we found in his car and apartment. He sent that letter to you. He thought Billy and you were an item, and I truly suspect you were in danger too," he held my hand and went on to say, "It's all over, Rose." I was shaking; Pat arrived, and she went to the kitchen to make some tea. She stayed with me overnight, and we talked and talked all night. I decided to take a few days off work to get my thoughts back in order again. Would it ever end for me? This entire trauma thing is getting to be too much.

The shooter was sent down for life with no parole. He pleaded guilty, so there was no actual trial.

Once again, I tried to put another nightmare behind me and pick up the pieces. Someone was looking out for me. Was it Nana or Kedrick?

Inspector Looney dropped by my house several times, over the next few weeks.

It was usually on a Saturday morning, and we had a cup of tea together.

He told me all about his marital woes, how his wife did not understand him.

He had three teenage boys, and they were having problems in school.

I said, "Marty," that was his name I found out, "it's a very stressful job being a mother to three boys, and I understand she is also a nurse; she really has her hands full. You both have to communicate more, and I'm sure you can work it out."

"Yes, I guess you are right," he replied.

I never encouraged him, and he stopped dropping in a few weeks later.

I never heard from him after the hearings for sentencing was over.

After all this, I was so looking forward to my week with the girls: I needed that break.

We went away every year, and soon we would be picking this year's getaway.

Oh, I just cannot wait. I remembered another of my Nana's sayings, "Don't go through life waiting to be dust."

GIRLS' GETAWAY WEEK

Spring came and went, then it was nearly time for our summer vacation. Pat and Brenda came over with travel brochures, and we were to pick out a place to visit for our annual "Girls' Getaway Week."

We really had been to all the usual holiday places and resorts, and then Brenda said, "Let's go on a Shannon Cruise."

"Will you steer the boat?" I asked.

"No! We can hire a driver," she said.

"You are serious," said Pat. "Is there a brochure there for such a trip?"

We all looked through, and found a phone number to call, and they said they would mail out a brochure.

"Are we all agreed then?" said Brenda.

"I guess so," I replied.

We put in a call to the number, and asked them to send us out the brochure, and then we looked at the calendar, as we had to decide what week we were all free.

"I think it's wise if we wait until after the 12th of July," said Pat. "That's their marching week up North, and in case there is any trouble, and it spills over (our boat pickup was just near the border), let us wait a week after that," so we decided on the last week in July, just in case.

The brochure arrived a week later, and the girls came over to look through it, and book the trip. We filled out the reservation form. I wrote a check for the deposit, and we had to pay the balance seven days before departing. It was a six-night, seven-day cruise, leaving on a Sunday and returning on a Saturday.

The girls always paid me back, and we split everything three ways.

We also decided that jeans, tees, and a jacket would be the appropriate dress.

It would be casual dining at riverside pubs, and casual dancing in the evenings, so there was no need to pack anything formal.

The weeks flew by, and I had a business trip to Germany before then, and soon it was time for our "Girls' Getaway Trip."

We had to drive up near the border, and stay overnight at a hotel there, and pick up our boat on Sunday morning.

Our driver, guide, or whatever you called him was in his thirties and full of jokes. He kept cracking them all the time, a real witty guy.

He said his name was Billy; this gave me the shivers, because my friend that was killed, well, his name was Billy too.

We were sure we were in for a great week, once we got on our way.

We each had our own bunk, down below deck, and Billy slept up on top, near the engine.

We laughed and joked our way down the Shannon, and wined and dined at some of the best pubs. The entertainment each evening was great, very upbeat, and we met many tourists. I really felt good, and I was enjoying myself a lot.

Three days into our trip, we had got as far as Killaloe, and the next three days were to be our return part. We came down one side of the Shannon, and we would return back on the other side.

We stayed docked at Killaloe overnight and had dinner at a nice pub restaurant there.

I really could not drink anything; lately I was having stomach problems, especially if I had drink. I usually only had a glass or two of wine anyway, so I opted for a soda this night.

I saw Billy in a backroom talking to two men: a well-known businessman and a local politician. All three seemed to be in a deep conversation, and they did not even notice me when I got up to go to the ladies' room, and I had to pass right by them.

We had another great night, and the girls had quite a few to drink, so they giggled a lot.

Billy came over to us and asked if we would have another drink, and "How long more did we want to stay before we went back to the boat?"

I said, "Oh! I'm fine for drink, and I think the girls have had enough too, so we will head back as soon as this round is finished."

He said, "Okay! I will head back and have the steps down for you, and watch your step. I don't want to have to dive in and pull you girls out of the water if ya fall in."

We got back to the boat about thirty minutes later, and we went straight to our bunks.

We said our goodnights to Billy, and turned in for the night. The girls were out like a light. I guess there is nothing like a couple of drinks to get a good night's sleep.

I kept turning and tossing, and I lay awake for what seemed like hours.

I guess deep down I was thinking of my first boat trip in Cape Town, and what had happened there. This still troubled me, and it brought back some very painful memories. Some unanswered questions too.

Suddenly I heard voices up on deck, speaking very quietly, but I heard other noises like boxes being moved around as well. This lasted about twenty minutes or so, and then all went quiet, and shortly afterwards I heard Billy go to his bunk.

I did not sleep very much at all, and both girls were "out for the count" and never moved all night.

I was up early, before Billy even awoke, and I just sat looking out towards the pub.

It was not open yet, and we would not be moving on until we had breakfast there; that was the arrangement.

I noticed a large bulky heap over in the corner, covered with a tarp. "That wasn't there yesterday," I said to myself. Dare I go over to check? It was right beside where Billy was sleeping.

I heard the girls move downstairs, and this woke Billy up.

Forget it, I told myself, but I was "Curious Rose."

Soon we got off to get breakfast, Billy included, so I picked my moment.

Just as we all sat down, I said I had left my purse onboard, and I would go get it, and that I would be right back.

I ran down the jetty, jumped onboard, and went straight over to the bundle.

I lifted one corner of the tarp and saw several wooden boxes. I knew exactly what they were as I had seen them on TV recently when police had raided a known IRA sympathizer's house and found similar ones in his attic. They were guns: "AK-47s."

I quickly got back off the boat and headed back. Billy commented, "That was quick; you are out of breath." I replied, "I am starving, so I need food. I fancy some toast and perhaps some bacon."

I suddenly did not feel like eating, but forced myself to do so, in case anyone noticed that I was uptight and jittery.

We got back on the boat, and Billy pulled away from the jetty. The girls were all talk, and I took a book with me, and decided to sit on deck and read it.

I really did not read it as my thoughts were running wild. How could this be happening to me again? I had only been on a boat twice—the first time I suspected the owner of diamond smuggling, and now this, gun smuggling.

What I saw in the pub last night now fell into place. The well-known businessman and the politician were always suspected of being sympathizers, and rumor had it they were involved in "Gun Running" as it was sometimes called.

I will never get on another boat, ship, yacht, or even a canoe as long as I live.

What do I do now? Do I tell authorities?

I remembered Nana's advice again, "Hear, See, and Say nothing."

I would probably be a marked person if I spilled the beans, so I decided once again to take Nana's advice, at least for now anyway.

The trip back was much the same as the first leg, and I tried to keep up the pretence that I was having a great time. I also decided not to tell the girls until we got home. You never know, if they had a few drinks, they might say something to the wrong person.

We pulled in to the dock on Saturday evening on schedule.

We thanked Billy, and gave him a tip.

We were staying over at the hotel that night and heading back to the city after breakfast in the morning.

On the trip back, Pat said, "You are very quiet, Rose—are you okay?"

I started to tell them the story, and all I could hear from both was "no way," "you're kidding," "bloody hell," "what do we do?" I even heard what sounded like the "F" word a few times.

I very calmly said, "For now we do nothing."

"Brenda, is your cousin still a detective at the Castle?" I asked her.

"Yes! Why?" She answered.

I did not want to get involved with Marty Looney again. He was the inspector on Billy's case. In addition, I had remembered that Brenda had a cousin as a detective.

"Well, let's invite him over in a week or so, and we will tell him what I saw, but it's on the condition that the tip remains anonymous," I said.

"There is no way we could ever give our names; can you imagine, court cases for months, even years. We would be called on as witnesses, and probably put on a death list by the gunrunners."

"I still can't believe you saw that," said Pat.

"Are you questioning what I saw?" I said to her.

"Oh! God no, just why our boat?" she said.

"They probably do it on more than one boat; it's the perfect cover. Tourists enjoying themselves, and most with a few drinks at night, so they sleep soundly," I said.

The rest of the journey home was quiet; none of us said much.

Every so often one or the other of the girls would say, "Bloody hell, it had to happen to us," or "I can't believe this has happened to us."

I said, "Let's put this at the back of our minds for now, and ring your cousin in a week or two and set up a meeting at my house or yours. It's more private that way. Do not tell him what it is about, just in case he says something or lets it slip at work. The longer we leave it, the better it is for us; they will have forgotten us and won't suspect us."

I turned up the radio for the remainder of the journey, and like a jolt from the blue, there was our song "Strangers in the Night." It remained on my mind all the way home, and even after I dropped off the girls, and I had gone in to run a bath, I kept humming it. It was our song, but our ending was different.

That night I had a dream that Kedrick was alive and looking for me, and when I awoke, I realized it was just a dream, but it seemed so real at the time. I thought I could actually feel him and smell his cologne.

Thoughts started running through my head. I had moved house; I moved jobs; my phone number was not listed, and those were the only places he could contact me.

I had not kept in touch with anyone from my old job or even any of my old neighbors.

I was out at work all day anyway, and I really did not know them very well, and my old work colleagues were a reminder of the golf tournament, so I kept away from them as well.

Pull yourself together, Rose; move on, I told myself. Keep the memories, but live your life.

I am sure that is what he would have wanted me to do. I kept saying this to myself over and over again, and then I had to get ready for work.

When I got to the office, all the staff asked how our trip went. I said, "It was very enjoyable. I would recommend it, if lots of partying and good food and having fun are what you need on a holiday. We had very little sleep and we met many nice folks from all around the world: German, Japanese, to name just a few nationalities. Yes, it was very interesting."

THE LONG, HOT SUMMER MONTHS

August flew by very quickly, and I only had one trip planned to London. People think you are having a great time with all this traveling to so many places. Well, the truth is, it becomes boring very quickly, because all you get to see is the limo to the airport, the limo to the hotel, and the limo to the office meeting. You probably had a business dinner that night and then back in the limo to the airport the next morning.

You really do not get to see any sites, just the inside of airports and hotels and limos, and to add to all that, you are jet-lagged and tired for a few days afterwards, but having said all that, "I love my job."

Brenda had asked her cousin the detective to drop over to her house on Friday night.

"Why did it take so long?" I asked her when she phoned to tell me.

"Oh! He was away on holiday for three weeks in August, so I only just contacted him today," she said.

I had nearly forgotten all about it, but as I said before, the longer the better for us, so that no one would connect us.

Pat and I went to Brenda's house on Friday, and we met her cousin. I had never met him before, but Pat had met him on a few occasions previously.

I did all the talking, and I got him to assure me that our names would never ever be mentioned.

When I had finished my story, he said, "Nothing new here, we have suspected those guys for months, but could never figure out how they transported them up North. We know they came into Limerick Dock, but the trail went cold from there."

"Well, now you know," I said.

He called me a few days later to say he had told his supervisor but did not give our names, saying it was an anonymous tip and they were putting a team in place to track the comings and goings of the businessman, the politician, and Billy the boatman.

That was the last I heard of it, and I felt I had done my job, so I tried to put it out of my mind.

I remember getting a phone call from my younger brother asking if he could stay with me for the weekend of the "All Ireland Football Final" our home county was playing.

"Could he also bring a few friends?" he asked.

"How many?" I asked.

"Oh! Just two or three," he said.

Well, he arrived on Saturday evening with four friends. The game was being played on Sunday at 2:00 p.m.

I told them they could sleep on my sitting room floor, and I gave them all blankets.

I knew they did not really want to sleep, just eat, smoke, and have a few beers.

I left them watching TV, and I went upstairs to bed around 10:30 p.m.

Suddenly the doorbell awakened me, along with a lot of noise downstairs, so I went to the top of the stairs and looked down, and five more of his friends had arrived.

"Oh well," I said to myself, "they will be gone tomorrow."

Little did I know then, I had to tell four of them to go home nearly a week later.

Every morning I went to work, they said they would be gone when I got back, but they were still there, so finally I had enough.

My brother had gone home on Monday morning after the game, so I knew none of the remaining guys.

My house was a mess. The smells of smoke, beer, and fried bacon and sausage was everywhere.

I had a word with him and he never did that to me again. He got the message, loud and clear.

I had to get my cleaning lady in to do a special cleanup for me.

My birthday was coming up soon, so my friends were throwing a party for me.

I was going to be thirty-three this year.

You were considered an "Old Maid" if not married by then, but I had my mind set on my career, and marriage was not in the cards for me.

I made lots of male friends, but I was very fussy whom I actually dated.

I had met one guy every morning in the car park at work. He worked as an engineer in the next office block, so we met nearly every morning, and we started talking, and I liked him a lot.

One morning he asked me if I was free that weekend to attend a function with him. I asked, "What is it for?" and he said, "It's a charity function for leukemia, a fundraiser actually."

I said, "Yes, I would love to go with you."

He arranged to pick me up at my place, and we drove together to the event.

He told me his sister had died from leukemia, and he was very involved in a charity to raise funds for this research.

I had a really nice evening, and in some ways, it was also sad, as it brought back memories of Kedrick's daughter Hannah, and of course Kedrick.

When he left me home, he asked if he could see me again and I said, "Yes."

Things were beginning to look up.

We dated a lot over the next few months, and I was getting to like him a lot.

He had a heart of gold, couldn't do enough for me. He was always giving me presents, and even gave me his checkbook with all the checks signed when he had to go overseas on a prolonged business trip, just in case I needed anything, and of course to pay his bills for him while he was away.

We had arranged to see a musical one night, and I had gotten the tickets, but he never showed up, and I could not get him on the phone. I went on my own, thinking he would meet me there. He never showed. "There has to be an explanation," I said to myself. That is not like him, but I had my doubts.

I did not see him for several weeks after that, and when I did, he just said, "I was called away on urgent business," giving me no other explanation.

I said, "Why didn't you telephone me?" I got no reply, just a shrug of his shoulders.

I saw him again a few times after that, but again he was very unreliable and was late or just never showed at all.

"I just do not have any luck with men," I kept saying this to myself repeatedly.

I was waiting in the car park one evening when a work colleague of his came over to me and said, "Did you know Louis is in the hospital?"

"No, what's the matter with him?" I asked.

"He was found unconscious in his garage last week; you do know he is an alcoholic?" he said.

177

"I did not know; I just knew he liked a few drinks, but I never saw him drunk."

"What hospital is he in?" I asked.

He told me, and I decided to visit Louis that evening.

He was very embarrassed when I showed up, and there were no other visitors there at the time.

I told him I would assist him in getting help when he got out, and we would work this out. I would help him in every way I could.

We talked a lot, and then I could not believe what he asked me to do.

"Will you drop out to the off-licence, and get me a pack of beer?" he asked.

I said, "Louis, we have spent the last hour talking about getting you help, and this is not what I meant."

I refused to get him any. I guess deep down he was relieved too. When you are dependent on something, it must be very difficult to say no. I had to say it for him.

He spent two weeks in the hospital. I visited him regularly, and I was there for him when he got out. He told me he had a brother in Belfast and that he had arranged for him to enter a treatment facility up there, and he would contact me when he got back.

I never heard from him after that, and when I called his brother, he told me he had gone to Canada to see another brother, and that he was still in treatment.

It had been also discovered, during some tests, that he had a heart condition, and this is why he went to Canada to seek medical help there.

Months later, I got a phone call from his brother in Belfast saying he had passed away from his heart condition, and I suppose his other problem did not help either.

I sent flowers, but did not attend his funeral. It was another painful event that I was running away from, and again I began to question if there really was a God.

Again, Nana's words came to mind: "There is a reason for everything."

THE BIRTHDAY PARTY

The party was fun; it was held in a local restaurant, in a private room at the back.

I was surprised to see Brenda's cousin there, the detective, and he seemed to be hanging on to Pat. They seemed very close; was there something going on?

I asked her later if they were dating and she said, "Yes, I was out with him last week, and he wanted to come tonight. He is cute; don't you think so?" She asked.

"Yes! He seems real nice, and I wish you both the very best," I said.

I really meant it. Pat was thirty, and she really wanted to settle down, as for Brenda, well, she was in a relationship for years, but it did not seem to be going anywhere.

I was always telling her to move on, and she used to say, "Look who's talking about moving on."

She always went back to him. At least she had someone to go back to.

Brenda's cousin, Ted, came over to wish me a "Happy Birthday."

He whispered into my ear, "We got the goods on you know who." I just nodded and said, "I'm glad I was of some help."

(The court case was on for years, and many heads were rolling, as it involved a large number of well-known people.) I felt justice was done, and that I had played a very minor part in it.

I came home that night and just could not get to sleep. Every time I closed my eyes, I saw Kedrick, but when I opened them, it was just dark. My alarm clock light shining on my bedside table was the only light.

I need help to get me through this, I thought, *it has been going on too long.*

I made a mental note to talk to my doctor as soon as possible, and to see what he would recommend.

AUTUMN LEAVES

I had tons of trees in my back garden, and I spent every weekend sweeping up the leaves.

"I really must get someone to do this," I said to myself. I had terrible allergies from the dust.

My neighbor had someone do it for them, so I asked them to send him over to me.

He was a "godsend." He took care of everything for me. I found out he was actually a teacher, and he did this in his spare time. His name was Joe, and he brought his son with him sometimes. He was a real nice kid, about nine or so.

Told me he got all "A's" in school. I said, "Your parents must be very proud of you."

He said, "My mother is dead; she died last year of cancer."

I said, "I am so sorry. I did not know," and I gave him a big hug.

I asked Joe later what had happened and he said, "One day she was fine, and the next she was in the hospital with severe stomach pain, and when they operated, they just closed her back up, as she had last-stage stomach cancer. We had just come back from our Greek holiday, so we thought it was some bug or other she picked up. She died six weeks later.

It was very hard on my son, Toby; we only have the one child. I miss her terribly," he said.

I could see the tears in his eyes. Is there really a God, I questioned.

Joe was wonderful; he took such good care of my garden and my roses, and we always had a cup of tea and a long conversation each time he came. We became very good friends.

Late one Thursday night, I got a phone call from Mam. She said that Dad had been taken to the hospital, as he had chest pains, but initial tests said it was not his heart. They are keeping him in for further tests, and he will be there a few days.

I said, "I will drive down in the morning," but she said, "No! Wait until we get the results from the tests. He is fine now."

"What ward is he in?" I asked her.

"St. Rita's," she answered.

"Okay. I will ring there in the morning to check on him," I said.

Turned out it was an ulcer he had. He was put on medication and is as good as new now.

He gave us all a shock. I do not know what I would have done if I'd lost my dad.

A shudder went through me, and I thought, *Am I to lose all the important men in my life?*

I went to bed that night, and I had another dream about Kedrick.

"I just have to go back to Cape Town," I said to myself when I got up, next morning.

I just have to—that is the only way I can get closure.

I realized that no doctor could help me. I had to do it myself; I just had to go back.

MY NEIGHBOR

My elderly neighbor Ellie was a real dear. I loved to listen to her stories. She lived alone and was considering moving into assisted living. I invited her for tea one evening, and she told me the story of her life. She had lived in this house since childhood. She was born there and had taken care of her parents and her brother in this house. You could see the gleam in her eyes as she spoke about her family and her home.

The house was real Old World. With wooden beams all over the place, it was beautifully decorated in earth shades. She had lace curtains on her windows, just like mine, and she had commented on this when I first met her. Joe had been taking care of her lawns since he was a schoolboy, so I felt secure in having him do mine.

She told me that she was the youngest of six children, and when she was just sixteen, her mother had a stroke. She had to stay home to take care of her. She read books and educated herself, and she could be regularly found at the local library. She never married. She had boyfriends, and some were serious, and she did have some marriage proposals, but her dedication to her parents and siblings always came first. I came to really love and admire Ellie. She always inquired about cousins Sally and Betty, the ones from Boston.

You could talk to her on any subject, and she was always up to date with whatever was in the news; she had her own opinion on everything. I often wondered what she would have become if she had gone to college.

When I had to travel, she took in my mail and kept an eye on my home. She became like a second Nana to me. I met her nephews and nieces, and they were all so polite and kind to me as well. She had a real nice family. I would miss her if she did indeed go to assisted living.

She even hinted that Joe would be a good match for me; I gave it the deaf ear, for now anyway.

NEW YEAR'S CELEBRATIONS

December 19th came around, and as I had done for every year since the plane crash, I went to church, and said a prayer for Kedrick and Hannah, and of course my grandparents and my friend Billy.

The thoughts were as fresh in my mind today as they were that awful day in October when his plane crashed. It was like a still-life picture etched in my mind.

I spent Christmas with my family, and came back to the city for the New Year.

I was invited to a New Year's Party, so I got out a nice dress, and met up with some friends before we headed to the party.

It was held in a very posh hotel, and about three hundred people were there to celebrate the New Year.

I knew some people there, and I had a really nice time, and the food was superb.

We all joined hands at midnight and sang "Auld Lang Syne."

I danced my heart out, and I felt good.

What did the New Year have in store for me?

I did not get home until after 3:00 a.m., and I slept most of New Year's Day.

I had no plans for dinner; actually, I just wanted time alone.

Late afternoon the phone rang and a male voice said, "Is this Rose?"

I said, "Yes."

He said, "I am a friend of Piers in New York; my name is Don Wilde.

"I was with him last week, and he gave me your phone number to call you when I next visited Dublin. I will be flying in tomorrow for a week and I would like to take you out to dinner.

"What evening are you free?" He asked and then added, "Rose, a very Happy New Year to you."

"Thank you!" I said. "I am free most evenings this week. I do not travel very much in the winter months; do not want to be snowed in somewhere, especially not some airport.

"This happened to me a few times when I first started traveling with this job. I am a wiser person now," I said.

We arranged to meet at a well-known restaurant on Tuesday night at 7:30 p.m.

"How will I know you?" I asked.

He laughed and said, "I'll be wearing a 'Tam O Shanter,' you know the Irish cap—no seriously, just ask at the desk for my table. I will be there ahead of you."

Actually, the 'Tam O Shanter' is a Scottish cap, but I let him believe it was Irish.

"Fine, I'll see you there," I said. I hung up, and I immediately called Piers in New York.

"Who is this Don Wilde?" I asked. "And by the way, Happy New Year."

"Rose, I am glad he contacted you; he is from London, and a friend of mine. I had not seen him for a long time until he came to New York a week or so ago.

"You will like him, I think. He is an engineer, and he likes to go flying in his glider, and another thing, he is also very good looking." He said.

Piers and I chatted for a few minutes more, and he asked me when my next trip to New York was.

"March, I think, but I will let you know well before that, on the exact date," I said.

The office was all a buzz when I got in on Monday morning.

Two girls had gotten engaged over the New Year. There was only a few singles left, and I was the oldest of them.

I am sure they all felt sorry for me, but marriage was far from my mind right now.

THE COCKNEY

I met Don on Tuesday as arranged, and yes, he was good looking, very witty, and he seemed like a real nice person. We had a lovely evening, and he said, "Can I see you again before I go back on Saturday?"

We arranged to meet again on Friday, same time, same place. He walked me to my car, and asked me for the keys to open the door, and I felt a shiver go through me, and immediately I put the key in the lock myself and opened it. He kissed me on the cheek as we said goodnight.

I felt a chill come over me.

Driving home, I thought, *Not bad, could be interesting.*

Piers knew me so well; he knew I would like him.

Friday came; we met for dinner, and again it was a very enjoyable evening.

He had such an interesting life; he traveled a lot too, and even suggested that he stay at my place, next time he came to town.

Very quickly I said, "My parents come up regularly, and sometimes they arrive unexpectedly, so I don't think that would be a good idea."

I did not like this familiarity so quickly in the relationship.

I had only just met him.

He said, "I'm sorry if I seemed to be rushing things, but I would like to see you again. I come over at least twice a month."

I said, "Don, that's fine with me; we can meet up and have dinner, that's if I'm in town, and then we have to take it slowly from there."

"I understand. Piers mentioned you had a great loss in your life," he said.

"More than you will ever know, and even now years later, it's very difficult to talk about it, so that's why I need to take things slowly, very slowly," I said.

"I fully agree with you, and I totally understand your position," he said as he walked me to my car, and he kissed me full on the lips. I did not respond.

"I will call you when in town next time. Good-night," he said, and I started up the engine and said, "Okay! See you then, and have a safe trip home, and thanks for the lovely evenings we have had together."

"It's been a real pleasure...," he said, and I drove off even before he had finished.

I liked his company, but I just could not put my finger on it, something did not ring true.

Was I just being "Curious Rose" again?

I had asked him on that first evening if he was married, and he had answered that he was not married; he was too busy with his career.

He told me all about his family, his parents, and two sisters, yet deep down something bothered me. He really could have been describing any family, no intimate details at all.

"There I go again," I said to myself. I had once read a saying and it came to mind: "If you want to go fast, you go alone. If you want to go far, you go with others."

I really must make the effort to be more trusting of others; otherwise, I will end up on the fast track, all alone.

TEMPUS FUGIT

Life continued on, lots of traveling, many casual dinner dates, but nothing serious; therefore, I began to shop a lot, every weekend. I was always the best dressed at every gathering. Nana had taught me well.

I was to find out much later that this was just something to do mainly to occupy my time, and I guess it also filled a void in my life. It was also dipping into my savings, big time.

I met Don several times over the next year, and I was getting to like him a lot, but deep down something was holding me back.

Was it woman's intuition or was it telepathy and a sense that it was not right?

I just do not know. I realize I was unfair to most of my dates; I just kept comparing them to Kedrick.

One night he had asked me to accompany him to a function, where I met some of his business associates. He introduced me to them, and then went to the bar to get some drinks.

I was still having stomach problems, especially if I had a drink, so when he asked what I would like, I said, "Just chilled water, please Don."

I sat at the table with some of his associates and chatted to them, mostly about the weather, and of course the Dublin sights.

I could see Don chatting to one of them up at the bar. He was up there for a very long time, so I excused myself, and I got up to go to the ladies' room.

As I left, I overheard a comment, "I wonder, does she know that he is getting married to Lady Pamela next month?"

I heard laughter and then a voice said, "Oh boy! I do not know how he gets away with it; he is a real womanizer." I kept on going to the ladies' room, and I even considered just leaving, but my wrap was back at the table.

I felt faint, so I got a glass of water in the ladies' room, and I just sat there while I tried to gain my composure, and get my thoughts together.

I took my time, and I had decided how to handle this tricky situation by the time I got back to our table.

When I returned, he was already seated, and he said, "I was just going to look for you; what took you so long?"

"Oh! I ran into an old boyfriend of mine in the hallway and we just chatted over old times." (I was smiling while saying this white lie, and I do not even know why I said it.)

He just looked at me, and he was silent. I could see he was irritated.

I was all talk for the rest of the night to all the other people at our table.

We left the function, and I was supposed to go back to his hotel with him for a nightcap, but I told him I would just like to go home.

I looked straight at him and said, "Don, I think this is the end of the road for you and me. I need to move on."

He seemed shocked and said, "What brought this on—is it that old boyfriend you met?"

"Something like that," I said. "I am not the type who two times. I am a one-man woman, and I need to have a good look at my life and I have to decide what to do for the future; you see, my biological clock is ticking." I also needed to check out the facts before I said anything to him about what I had overheard. Deep down, I knew it was true.

I walked to my car, and he came with me. I opened the door to get in, and he leaned forward to kiss me, and I just turned my cheek to him.

I said, "Don, I wish you good luck, and I hope you find happiness in whatever it is you do with your life."

"May I call you next time I am in town?" He asked.

"If you want, but it's just to talk. I will not be meeting you," I said.

I drove off, leaving him standing there with a puzzled look on his face.

I would tell him why, later, the reason for my actions, if he rang me.

I would ring Piers next day and see if he knew what was going on.

Meantime I got my say in first, and I had given him the boot.

I felt very pleased with myself, but deep down, I also felt sad and I felt betrayed, and that hurt, as I did like him a lot. It just was not right from the start; something was missing.

Next day at lunch break, I phoned Piers, and he said, "I was going to call you when you got home tonight."

I said, "That's nice; are you coming to visit me?"

"Not just yet, have you seen Don lately?" he asked.

"Yes! Last night in fact, we attended some function of his, and I met some of his work associates."

There was a slight pause and then he asked, "How are things with you two?"

"It's really nothing serious; actually I told him last night I wouldn't be seeing him again, and that I was moving on with my life," I replied.

"Rose, you don't know how glad I am to hear you say that, as I have some news for you. I have not spoken to him for over six months, and last night I read an article in a British newspaper that some

Lord's daughter was getting married next month to a "Don Wilde." I don't know of any other Don Wilde with a similar bio; all the facts were of him.

"Did he say anything to you?" He asked.

"No," I replied, "and it's water under the bridge now, and I am moving on."

"I felt I needed to tell you as I was the one that introduced you to him. I was so afraid you would get hurt again, after all you have been through, and I would not wish to have anything like that happen to you. You are a very special friend, Rose," and he went on to ask when my next trip to New York was being scheduled. "Within two months," I replied. "I have some issues to resolve with a company in Manhattan."

"Be sure to call me beforehand, and we can set up a dinner date. I am so looking forward to seeing you, Rose, and think positive—things usually turn out right if you keep moving forward," he said.

"Thanks, Piers. I'll do that, now you take care," and I hung up.

That night I had another dream about Kedrick. I did not have any for a while, and now I was having them regularly.

This time we were on a flight to Cape Town, and he was sitting beside me, just holding my hand.

When I awoke, I was in my own bed, and again it was just a dream, but it seemed so real.

The years were flying by, and my stomach was getting worse, so I decided it was time to do something about it.

I went to my parents' home for the weekend, and I noticed they had slowed down a lot, but thankfully, they were still in good health, and Dad never had any problems from his ulcer since he started his treatment.

I told them I was going to make an appointment to see a specialist about my stomach.

Mam said, "I didn't know you had stomach problems?"

"Yes, I have been having some problems lately," I told her.

"It's wise to have it checked out; as you know, stomach cancer runs in your dad's family," she said.

"Thanks Mam, I needed that," I replied.

"No Rose, I am serious; the earlier things are found, the better the prognosis, and it's probably just an ulcer anyway, just like your dad, treatments are much better nowadays," she said.

"Okay, please, let's change the subject," I said.

I felt better after the visit with my parents, as they were very supportive to me in whatever I did with my life.

I drove back to the city on Sunday afternoon and kept switching radio stations, and not once, but twice, our song "Strangers in the Night" came on the radio.

I made up my mind there and then that it was time for that trip to Cape Town, and then and only then would I get closure. It had been ten years since that plane crash.

I got to bed late that night because I knew I would not sleep much; I had too many things on my mind.

My intention was to ask my boss Fergal if I could take a month off, as I wanted to visit South Africa, and if I did not do it now, I would probably never get to do it.

He knew my story; he was an old friend, and we had no secrets. I think that is why we got on so well together, but I did work hard for him too. He got his money's worth, and I did do a good job. He appreciated this very much, and it means a lot sometimes to have your boss just say 'Thank You.' Those two words can be very rewarding, and they are not said enough nowadays.

Looking back, he was probably the best boss in the world, very considerate and understanding, worth his weight in gold. He was totally dedicated to his family.

I decided to postpone my doctor's visit until I got back from Cape Town.

With all this clear in my mind, I settled down to try to get some sleep, and eventually I did fall asleep.

I was up early and had a good breakfast, and headed into work with all my plans.

It was now September, and on the last Sunday in October, it would be the tenth anniversary of Kedrick's plane crash. I had to find closure—it was time.

I read the newspaper while I waited for Fergal to come in.

THE PROPOSITION

He came rushing in and said, "Rose, I need to see you straight away in my office."

(*Hell, what have I done now*, I thought to myself.)

I could not recall anything, so I went into his office.

He was all excited, and said, "I have a proposition for you, Rose; this all happened over the weekend, and I think it's right up your alley."

I said, "What? What? What?"

"Okay! Let's start at the beginning," and he began by telling me that it was confirmed 100% that we were opening a branch office in New York on January 31st.

"Jerry, one of our sales managers will run it, but I need someone with a financial background there as well, and I think, actually I know, you are the right person.

"It would be for a two-year period initially, and I think it's just what you need in your life right now—a new challenge," and he went on and on, until finally I got a word in.

"Actually I had planned to talk to you this morning anyway," I said, and I proceeded to tell him my plan.

"Rose, our largest customers out of the New York office will be all the South African Airlines, and I can arrange some trips over there for you; that way you can combine business with pleasure, tag on a few days' vacation to your trips, and do whatever it is you need to do. It's perfect for you, Rose, please say yes."

He asked in such a nice way. He had all that charm.

I said, "Let me sleep on it, and I will let you know in the morning."

Now I really was in a tizzy. I called everyone I knew that night and asked his or her advice.

Most said, "Go for it."

My mother had some reservations and said, "Rose, you need to have your stomach problems checked out first."

"They have all the latest tests over there," I said.

Then I thought, *Well they have them here now too, and with all the new clinics opening, maybe it's better if I did have it checked out here. I do love my doctor and he really cares.*

She went on to say, "You would have no one to take care of you over there, so think it over very carefully."

"I will sleep on it, Mam," I said. I waved goodbye, and I sat into my car for the trip home.

By morning I had already made up my mind which way to go.

Was it west to New York, or south to South Africa?

I went to church and prayed for Kedrick and Hannah on the last Sunday in October, and again on his birthday, the 19th of December.

I spent Christmas and New Year's with my family, and headed back after the holidays to start my packing for my trip or adventure, as some people called it.

My neighbor Ellie was standing outside her door as I drove in my driveway.

"Is everything all right, Ellie?" I asked her.

"Yes Rose, but I have news for you," she replied.

"Okay, let me park and I'll come right in to you," I said.

I followed her into her house; we sat in the kitchen, and she told me that she had decided to go into assisted living at the end of the month. "I talked it over with my family, and we all think it's the best thing for me. My nephew Bob is coming to live here. He is married to Betty, and they have two grownup children; you know them, you have met them." She had a tear in her eye as she said this to me.

I hugged her and said, "Ellie, I think it's probably the best thing for you too," and I went on to tell her that I myself would be leaving to go overseas as well.

She made me a cup of tea, and I told her to let me know her plans.

We hugged, and I made my way back home. I had a lot of thinking to do.

END OF AN ERA

Ellie stood on the lawn outside her home; her frail body looked as if it could be knocked over by a breeze. Her nephew Bob was there to take her to her new home.

Her long white hair was piled high on top of her head. She wore a high-neck blouse with a mid-length skirt, always elegant. This morning she had her beaver coat wrapped around her. A wool hat was pulled down over her eyes to try to hide the tears that were there. You see, it was the last time she would turn the key in the door of this home; she was going into an assisted-living facility just a few miles away. She had been putting it off for over a year. I heard Bob ask, "Ellie, are you ready?"

"Yes, but I want to hug Rose first," she replied.

I came over, gave her a big hug, and told her that I would keep in touch with her.

Bob helped her to his car, and as she regained her composure, I could hear her tell him, "Now young man, you drive carefully."

Bob just laughed as he sat in. I waved, as did some of the other neighbors who had also come out to see her off. She grinned and said, "I feel like the Queen." She started to wave back, just like the Queen. "Good ol' Ellie," I said to myself.

DID I DO THE RIGHT THING?

I felt someone shake my shoulder, and the steward-ess said, "Madam, fasten your seatbelt, and put your seat back up as we are preparing to land.

"You must have been really tired; you slept all the way, and the flight is nearly an hour late due to very strong headwinds."

The captain came on, and it was a woman. "We should be at the gate very shortly," she said. "Welcome to JFK, New York. Your time here is 3:00 p.m., and the temperature is a cool 48F. Enjoy your stay here and thank you for flying with us today."

I cleared immigration and customs, and I came outside to see Piers waiting for me.

I had called him when I had decided what I was going to do, and he said there was an apartment in his building for lease, and did I want him to check it out for me.

I told him to go ahead as it would be nice to have someone nearby that I knew.

"Okay," he said, "I'll get on it straight away. Are you restricted with rent?" He asked.

"Not really," I said, "but do keep it within reason. The company is paying for the first three months anyway."

He sent me a picture by express mail, and it looked real nice and clean.

He said it was the reverse floor plan to his, and I knew his floor plan, as I had visited him there several times over the years. I had no hesitation and said, "Go ahead; reserve it for me, and I will wire you the money tomorrow. Give me your bank details."

He told me there was no need for that, "You can pay me back when you get here."

"I'd prefer to send the money, Piers," I said.

"Okay! If that's what you want," he said, and he spelled out all the details for me.

He was the one that suggested that he would pick me up at JFK. I told him the company would do that, and he said, "It's not a problem, and I know the way to my own apartment, so it would make sense. Right, Rose? There, it's all settled," he said. "See you at Kennedy."

"Well, here I am," I said, as I walked towards him.

He gave me a kiss and a hug and said, "Rose, this is so great you being here. I know you will like it, and it's also a new beginning for you," and he picked up my two blue cases, and we headed out to the parking lot.

I thought to myself as I walked beside him, *A new beginning, a new life, and hopefully a new me. What does life have in store for me now?*

I know I will always have my memories.

THE APARTMENT

The apartment was sparsely furnished, and I found out later most apartments come unfurnished. Back home it is very rare to find something unfurnished.

I also found out Piers had bought me a new bed, and had purchased some items from the previous tenant. I needed the basic things for now. I would pay him back later.

"We can go furniture shopping on the weekend," he said, "but if you need anything, just come knock on my door. Your trunk arrived, so I had it put in the spare bedroom, and when you have it unpacked, I will put it into your storage space for you.

"Do you want to eat tonight, or do you just want to relax and get to bed early?" He asked.

"Also, remember, you gained five hours, so you will be out of sync until your clock adjusts. Is there anything else you need before I leave, as I have a few phone calls to make, and I'll call you later to see what you have decided to do," he said.

"I'll just have some tea (I had brought some with me), but I need milk and bread," I said.

"Look in your fridge; I have already taken care of it," he replied.

Sure enough, the fridge was full.

He had purchased milk, bread, cheese, orange juice, and all the necessary things to keep me going until I got out food shopping.

"You're a sweetheart, and we can catch up on all the news tomorrow," I said.

"When do you actually start work?" he asked.

"Not until a week from Monday next, they gave me time to get settled," I said.

"Oh! By the way I had a phone installed for you; this is your number," and he handed me a piece of paper. "It's ex-directory, but you can change that if you want," he said.

"You think of everything—just like a woman," I laughed.

"Yes! I have had plenty of experience living on my own," he said.

We talked some more and he stood up and said, "Call me if you need anything."

He kissed me on the cheek and said goodnight, and I was on my own.

I was in a strange apartment, a new country, a new job, and I had very few friends here.

Did I do the right thing?

I guess time will tell, and I went to look for my trunk.

CHOICES IN LIFE

Did I do the right thing? I kept asking myself this question repeatedly.

A little voice kept saying, "You will be fine, be strong."

Life is a series of choices; you choose one that suits you, and again I remembered something Nana used to say, "There is a reason for everything."

For me, well, only time will tell what that reason is.

I started to unpack some things, and I made some tea.

I made up my bed with my white cotton lace-trimmed sheets that I had shipped ahead in my trunk. I also took out a quilt that Nana had made for me when I first left home.

At least I had some of my favorite things around me.

I did fall asleep eventually, but the noise was something. I was not used to this, but I guess I will get used to it in time.

I awoke at some crazy hour; at first, I had to really concentrate as to where I was, it was no dream, and I really was in New York.

I spent the day checking out the apartment, and I called home to say I had arrived and that I was okay, and I also gave them my new telephone number.

Piers was taking me out to dinner that night, so I showered and put on a nice dress, and I was all ready when he called for me.

We had a wonderful dinner, and he gave me many tips on what to do and what not to do.

He told me I had a parking space allocated to my apartment, which I found out later is worth a fortune in New York.

I told him the company was supplying me with a car, but that would not be until next week; they were concerned as to where I could park it.

"This should put their minds at ease," I said.

Piers went on to plan out what I needed to do.

He said, "Tomorrow we will go to Macy's, so make up a list of what items you need, like furniture, utensils, etc., and they can make one delivery with everything.

"You will also have to go to Motor Vehicles within thirty days. I think it is thirty days anyway—to get your driver's license.

"I understand the company was able to get you a work visa so everything is above board, and you should have no problems."

After dinner, we walked to my door and he saw that I was inside before he left to go down to his apartment. "Don't open the door to anyone unless you know who is there; you do have an intercom, so please use it," he said to me before he left.

I said, "Piers, don't scare me," and he replied, "Rose, I just want to make sure you are okay. Remember, you are a very special person to me. Sleep well, and I will see you in the morning," and he kissed me on the lips, a very casual one.

We had arranged to meet early in the morning for our shopping trip.

I had no radio in my apartment, so that was the first item I put on my list.

I also needed an iron, ironing board, and some small items, but I needed furniture for my spare bedroom, a bed and bedside tables, and a coffee table for the sitting room.

I did not want to go overboard, as I would have to get rid of them if I wanted to go back in two years.

Piers came by, as promised, and we got a cab to Macy's.

I picked up everything I needed, and more as well; things I could not resist.

I arranged to have everything delivered on the following Tuesday, so I had nearly a full week to get everything sorted out.

I had arranged to meet my new work colleagues on Thursday and have lunch with them, and they were taking me to see my new office before I started work there on the following Monday.

They had arranged to pick me up and come see my apartment to make sure I was okay, and in a good neighborhood.

Piers said he would come by on Tuesday to help sort out my Macy's deliveries; hopefully they would keep their word and deliver as scheduled.

He was working over the weekend, so he had to leave as soon as we got back from shopping. "Call me if you need anything," he said and left.

BIG CITY LIFE

Life slowly began to fall into place, but I was homesick, and I kept questioning my decision.

My colleagues were very helpful, two of them I had known from previous visits, and of course, I knew Jerry, our manager. They were also very impressed with my apartment, and wondered how I had found it.

Our office overlooked Times Square, and we would have approximately twenty staff there eventually, the manager had told me.

My job was to send weekly reports back to the head office, and to continue to monitor my old accounts. I would also have to travel to keep up to date with my customers' needs.

I had my own office, so I decided to purchase a small radio, as I liked to work with the radio in the background. It never bothered me or interfered with my work.

My car was delivered to my apartment, and thankfully, it was a small sports type, therefore easy to park.

I did have my own parking space, both at the apartment and at the office, but I was unsure if I would use it during the week. I might just get the subway to work, and use the car on the weekends only.

It was an automatic, and I had always driven a stick shift, so I needed time to get used to it.

I also had to get used to driving on the other side of the road.

I had cousins in Boston, Chicago, and Connecticut, so I promised Mam and Dad that I would try to visit with them all, in due course, time, and weather permitting.

It was now June, and it was getting hot and sticky in New York. I did not go out much to socialize. Mam said I should try to get to see Sally and Betty soon as time was running out for them.

I met with some old friends from my previous trips, and we had dinner at least once a month. Some nights I felt I wanted to go back home. I really missed my home, my rose garden, and of course my family and friends. I think I was in some kind of depression.

Piers dropped by at least once a week, and we had our usual dinner date, once a month as well.

My apartment was on the fourth floor, and his was on the second, so I really did not see him come or go, or see any of his visitors.

I kept in regular contact with my girl friends, especially Pat and Brenda in Dublin.

They kept me up to date with all the news.

Pat informed me she was hoping to be engaged to Ted on July 26th (her birthday).

In July, Head Office contacted me to schedule a trip to Johannesburg the first week of August, if that was convenient to all parties involved. I had to check out their availability first.

I had made all the arrangements, and I had tagged on five days' vacation to fly down to Cape Town to finalize some "unfinished business" I had there.

That night I kept thinking about my last conversation with Kedrick. "Meet you in Paris" kept running through my head. Those were his last words to me.

I had my case all packed, and two days before I was due to fly, I came down with something. I was feeling nauseous, dizzy, and just felt terrible.

One of the girls from the office took me to her doctor. I had an inner ear infection, a very serious one, and I could not travel, so I had to cancel my trip.

I was in bed for three days, and I just listened to the radio (with my good ear) all the time. Television bothered me, all those ads. I just got so frustrated trying to watch something, perhaps I would get used to this too, all in time. It certainly was a completely new culture for me to get used to.

Every day, for those three days, our song, "Strangers in the Night," was played several times.

Again, my thoughts ran wild; is there a message here? Am I missing something? On the other hand, am I going crazy? Will I ever get to Cape Town?

I went back to work after the three days, but I still felt very weak, so I called the doctor.

I felt comfortable with this doctor; she was caring, and took her time with me. You were not just a number to her; you were treated like a human being.

I set up an appointment for the following week for a full checkup.

Pat called to say she had her ring, and they had set a date for their wedding: February fourteenth, St. Valentine's Day. *How romantic*, I thought.

"You better come home for it," she said. "Rose, I want you in my bridal party."

I was so excited for her, and she deserved it. I told her, "Yes, I promise you, I will be there, Pat."

I went to my doctor's appointment, and she said all looked fine. I mentioned to her I had some stomach problems, and she prescribed some medication for me to take.

"I want to see you again in a month, and if you are not feeling any better, I will have to send you for some tests." She asked for my medical history from Ireland, so I told her I would have them on my next visit.

August was very hot and sticky in New York, very uncomfortable. My doctor told me to continue the medication for another month, and she would review my records for my next visit.

A crowd of us went out to Long Island every weekend. One of my colleagues, her parents, had a summer home there on Fire Island near the beach, so we stayed there overnight, and we got back late on Sunday evenings. The traffic back to the city was a nightmare; each Sunday, cars were bumper to bumper.

It was party after party, and one night I just said to myself, "This is not you, Rose; it's all so superficial."

Once the weather cools down, I will go to Boston and Connecticut to visit with my relatives.

For the Chicago trip, I will probably have to fly there.

I arranged to travel to Connecticut and spend Labor Day weekend there.

I had a great time, and my cousin told me he would fix me up with a nice man next time I came to visit.

I said, "Make sure he has all his own teeth and a lot of money," and we both laughed. I felt so at home with my cousins, and I was laughing once again. The cousins here were on my father's side of the family.

Late September, when I was to reschedule my trip to South Africa and as I was preparing to make all the arrangements, Jerry came rushing into my office and said, "Rose, we cannot do any business with South Africa anymore, as some 'Trade Embargo' or other has been put on trade between this country and theirs. I don't know all the details as yet, so hold off on any travel trips for now."

He seemed upset, and my heart sank. I did not understand politics, and had no clue as to what this meant.

To me, it meant I was not going to Cape Town.

I can recall Nana at election time back home, every time a politician came knocking on her door to canvass her vote, she would send them away, saying, "You are all full of politician's pie. I will make up my own mind."

I asked her what "politician's pie" was, and she replied, "Full of hot air."

I guess that was to influence my interest in politics, which is absolutely none.

Once again, I felt cheated, as the main reason I had taken this job in New York was to get the trips to South Africa.

I left the office that evening with a heavy heart, and I felt very homesick.

The following week, just as I was to leave the office one evening, Jerry came in and said, "Rose, we are invited out on a dinner cruise next week. One of our customers owns a large yacht, and he entertains his clients onboard. This time it is for his bankers, so he needs all the support he can get in order to obtain a large line of credit for his company.

"Will you come with me?" he asked.

"Jerry," I answered in a firm voice, "I will never set foot on a boat again; it's just not for me." (Was he feeling sorry for me, and was this his way of making up for the cancelled South African trip?)

"Oh! Please do come with me; you get on with everyone, and my wife Carrie is in London, visiting her mother."

"I can't. I just can't, Jerry, and I would only get sick. Get one of the other girls to go," I said.

"Think about it, and sleep on it; you might feel different in the morning, Rose," he said.

Next morning he was waiting in my office for me, and he looked so pathetic that I gave in.

"Okay, I'll go, but it's straight home afterwards," I said.

The cruise was from 3:00 p.m. until 6:00 p.m. along Long Island Sound.

It went off very well, and I met many bankers, but I was glad when we docked and I got off and went straight to my car, having first said goodnight to Jerry.

"Whew! Thank goodness, we had no incidents; maybe the curse is broken," I said to myself.

Two days later, I nearly had a panic attack; the big headlines on the front page of all the newspapers read: "Two bankers arrested for insider trading, and embezzlement."

I had spent some time talking to both of them on the cruise.

That is it: Never again. I do not care who asks, job or no job, my nerves could not stand it.

A CHANCE ENCOUNTER

One evening, later in the week, I stopped at the local "deli" to get a take-a-way, and I had to stand in line for at least ten minutes. I ordered my sandwich, and I was just leaving, when I bumped into a tall, dark, handsome person.

He said, "I am so sorry; are you okay?"

"I'm fine, thank you," I said, and I started to leave when he asked me if I was Irish.

I said, "Yes, I am. Why?"

"I thought your accent sounded Irish," he said. "My family is Irish, and I go over there a lot. I go to visit my mother's family; they still live there."

"What part?" I asked.

"County Wicklow," he said.

"Very nice county, it's called 'The Garden of Ireland,' beautiful scenery there."

I moved towards the door and said, "Well, it's been nice meeting you; have a good evening."

"You too," he said, and I left and headed for home.

I went in and kicked off my shoes and bra, and changed into a lounge suit, and I sat down to eat my sandwich.

I turned on the TV to watch the news; all the usual were on: shootings, burglaries, the bankers' fraud, and of course sex scandals. It seems the media were obsessed with this, so I turned it off, and turned on my radio.

What do I do now? This question kept me awake all night.

I felt exhausted in the morning, so I called the office to say I was running late, as I had a bad night.

Somehow, I got through the day, and when I got home, I called my cousin in Boston, and arranged to spend Thanksgiving with her and her family.

I told her I would drive up and spend a few days with her and her family, and I was hoping I could get to meet all the "Boston Clan."

"We can't wait to see you," she said.

She gave me all the directions, and to call her if I got lost or was having trouble finding her house.

The week dragged by, and I had asked Jerry how long he thought this "Trade Embargo" would last. "Who knows, it could be months or even years, and of course it's a big loss to this office; business sales will be down, so I hope it is resolved real soon," he said.

"I hope so too, the sooner the better," I said.

The lease on my apartment was for twelve months, with an option for another twelve.

My contract here was for two years, so this arrangement suited me fine.

I decided I would renew the lease, and return home to Ireland after the two years were up.

I would finish out my contract here as I felt I owed my boss this after he had been so good to me.

The lease on my own home was also up in two years, so this fell into place very nicely.

I would give my tenants, two young accountants, six months notice over there that I would be returning home, and that I would need my home back.

I decided to hold off telling Fergal, my boss at the head office, or Jerry, in the Manhattan office, until much later.

I still had sixteen months left, so I had plenty of time. A lot can change in that time.

My doctor called to say she had reviewed my records, and told me she saw nothing urgent there, so I could continue taking the medication for another few months.

It was helping, so I went along with her advice.

My birthday was coming up, so Piers had asked me to accompany him to an art show, with dinner afterwards. I gladly accepted, as I always enjoyed his company and he was a very good friend. I had come to rely on him a lot, too much in fact. We were like an old married couple, without the strings attached.

The girls at the office also wanted to take me out to dinner, so we arranged that for the night before

Piers' art show. We had a fun time; I came to know them better, and we exchanged phone numbers.

The art show was lovely. I met many different people, and Piers is very popular I found out. He gave me a beautiful print for my birthday, and he said he would have it framed, but he wanted me to pick out the frame to suit my décor. I suspect he knew I was not going to stay in New York, and that I would be returning to my home when my contract was up. Piers knew me so well.

MEMORIES

The last Sunday in October came around, and as I watched the TV news that evening, a news flash appeared that a plane had crashed on takeoff at Palm Beach Airport.

The plane, carrying some golfers, crashed a few minutes after takeoff, but several survivors were found, and two bodies had also been recovered.

The survivors were seriously injured, and they had been taken to nearby hospitals where it was stated that most were suffering from severe burns. Further details would be available on the next update.

It re-opened my memories and the nightmares of that day now so long ago—was it now eleven years?

I was trembling; I just broke out into a sweat, and the tears came rolling down.

The memories and the pain were as fresh as if it had just happened.

When I get back to Ireland, I will take a month off, and take that trip to Cape Town.

I felt it was the only way that I could get closure.

I could not sleep at all that night, and I kept watching TV for the updates.

It was back to work as usual on Monday, and I really did not feel like cooking dinner, so I dropped in to my local deli, and I saw the good-looking Irish person there.

He said, "Hello Irish, how have you been?"

I said, "Great... and you?"

"Well, I have been very busy, but it is much better that way, and the days go by more quickly.

"I told my mother I had met an Irish girl, and she said she would love to meet you sometime. By the way, my name is Brian, Brian Kennedy," he said.

"Mine is Rose, Rose Kelly," I answered.

"Here is my card, Rose, and if you feel like Irish company anytime, just give me a call, and I'll arrange it," he said.

"Thank you, I appreciate that very much," I said.

I got my sandwich and put it in my bag. I put his card in my pocket, and wished him a nice evening, and I left.

The phone was ringing as I got into the apartment, and it was my friend Tim, the musician from Belfast. We still kept in touch, but not on a regular basis.

"Hi Rose! Guess what?" he said.

"What?" I asked.

"I'll be in New York for a week before Thanksgiving; is there any chance you can put me up?" He asked.

"Well, I'm driving to Boston for Thanksgiving, so what dates are you coming?" I asked.

He gave me the dates, and he would be leaving two days before I left for Boston.

"Okay, I'll make up a bed for you, and we can catch up on all the news," I said.

I told him to call me before he left, and I would pick him up at the airport.

"Thanks, Rose," he said. "I look forward to seeing you soon."

He really only wanted a bed for the few nights (I thought to myself), but I guess I owed him.

He had been a good friend to me over the years, but the romance part was cold. Yes, it was over.

The weeks flew by, and I had checked out my driving route to Boston, and how long it would take me to get there, so I was all set. I was looking forward to seeing my Boston Clan. The cousin is on my father's side of the family, and the two older women are on my mother's side.

Tim arrived; I met him at the airport, and I took him back to my apartment.

He seemed disappointed when I showed him his room, and I immediately told him I did not feel too good, so it was better if we had separate rooms.

I think he swallowed it, but the truth is, I just did not want to rekindle the relationship we once had. Been there, done that, and now it was time to move on.

We did have a really nice time, and I got caught up on all the home gossip.

His friend Karl from West Germany was also a musician, and he was meeting him at some studio the last day of his visit, so he asked me to have dinner with both of them that night.

"Sure! Where do you want to go?" I asked.

"I'd like you to choose, Rose, as I don't know any restaurants here, someplace nice," he said.

"Okay Tim, what time will I reserve the table for?" I asked.

"We should be well finished by 8:00 p.m., so book it for then," he said.

All three of us were sitting at the table reading our menus when I heard a voice say, "Well, if it isn't the Irish Rose," I looked up and there was Brian, the guy from the deli.

He had two older people with him, his parents I assumed.

I introduced him all around, and he introduced his parents to us as Kitty and Patrick Kennedy.

We chatted for a while and then he said, "We better take our seats or else someone will take our table."

As he left to go to his table, he whispered back to me, "Rose, please don't forget to call me sometime."

"Will do," I replied, and I went back to reading the menu.

Tim's friend Karl was a very nice person, and his English was also very good.

He told us his fiancée lived in East Germany, and he had been trying to get her out, as it was not a good situation over there. "Families are split, and it is very painful, but I will keep trying until I get her out.

"Her name is Ria," and he took out a picture from his wallet to show to me.

"She is very pretty," I said. "I wish you both all the luck in the world, and I hope it works out for you both. I'm sure it will be fine, just think positive Karl, and you know love always finds a way," I said.

The waiter came to take our order, and we enjoyed a nice meal.

We said our goodnights to Brian and his parents as we left the restaurant.

Karl took a taxi to his hotel, and Tim and I walked to my apartment, as it was only ten minutes away.

I had arranged a taxi for Tim in the morning to take him to the airport, as I had to work, and I had a very important meeting scheduled that morning.

In the morning, I made some tea and brought him a cup, as I had to leave before him, so I told him to lock up before he left. I gave him a hug and kiss, and said, "Tim, please do keep in touch," and I left.

I really have no feelings for him anymore; yes, no feelings, one way or the other, I thought to myself as I drove to work.

I guess I was moving on with my life.

THANKSGIVING IN BOSTON

This would be my first time to celebrate Thanksgiving. This holiday is not observed or celebrated in Ireland. Christmas and Easter, and of course Saint Patrick's Day, are the big holidays over there.

The drive to Boston went well, and I arrived at my cousins on Tuesday evening.

The fourth Thursday in November is always the Thanksgiving holiday—at least that is what I was told.

My cousin had arranged for all the family to come meet with me over the few days I would be there. I had also arranged to drive over to see Sally and Betty; they lived about one hour away from my other cousins. They appeared frail, particularly Betty. I met Betty's family, including her sons and daughter. Very welcoming, they invited me back to spend some time with them. "You have no excuse now; you are living here," said Sally. "Yes, and I promise I will be back," I told them. I drove the hour-long journey back to my other cousins for Thanksgiving. I was pleased that I had taken the time to visit with them.

We had a wonderful meal, and I also found out that turkey is the traditional dish.

Looking back, it was very similar to our Christmas holiday in Ireland: same meal, but of course, we had

Father Christmas, or Santa Claus as some call him, for the children.

This is what Christmas is all about—family and being together.

I remembered my neighbor Ellie, how good she had been to me, and we did keep in touch. Her letters were scarce now, as her writing was not that good, but I still felt she was always there for me, and was praying for me. So she told me in all her letters anyway. I think the reason I suddenly remembered her is that she made the best turkey and stuffing each Christmas.

It was fascinating to talk to everyone and listen to his or her opinions, and reminisce over old times. Most of us had grown up in Ireland, so we had played together as children, and of course, we had spent some time each summer at my grandfather's home.

I remember the saying, "Make new friends, but keep the old. The new ones are silver, but the old ones are gold." How very true.

Family and good friends are very important on this journey through life, and life is a journey. Nana and Ellie had always told me this.

I was also to learn a lesson later in life: you should never burn your bridges.

I got back to the city on Saturday evening, and just conked out on my couch.

I was exhausted from the driving and all that talking, and my cheeks were sore from all that laughing, and I also had very little sleep over the holiday. But it was great, and it gave me a great uplift.

I promised I would go back again very soon. I really meant it too.

I made all the arrangements to fly back to Ireland for Christmas, so I called my parents and told them I would be home for a short visit.

Mam asked me if I had been to see St. Patrick's Cathedral yet.

"Not yet, but I plan to go there on the 19th," I said.

I left work on the 19th and I went straight to St. Patrick's. I spent over an hour there, looking all around, and of course, I had several people to pray for.

I lit four candles, and picked up some leaflets to take home to Mam.

I dropped into my deli to grab a sandwich, and guess whom I met there—Brian.

I asked, "Do you come here often?"

He laughed, and said, "I usually come here to pick up a sandwich the nights I work the late shift."

I never did look at his card; I had just stuck it in my pocket, and I had forgotten all about it, so I did not know what he worked at.

We chatted for a few minutes, and he called after me as I left, saying, "Call me sometime as my mother keeps asking if I have seen you."

I came home and ate my sandwich, and then I searched for his card.

I could not remember what jacket I had on that night, but eventually I found it.

He was a doctor attached to the local hospital. I will call him soon, I said to myself, and I put his card on my coffee table.

I went Christmas shopping the next day to pick up some gifts to take home. I was flying out on the 23rd and back on the 28th.

It was a great Christmas, as all the family was back home, and they were so excited when I told them I would be returning home after my contract was up.

"This is the best present you could have given us," said Dad.

Mam asked if I had checked out my stomach problems and I said, "Yes."

I told her, "I am on medication, and I go back the end of January for further assessment."

I think that put her mind at ease. Do mothers ever really have peace of mind?

All too soon, it was time to fly back. I picked up a bottle of Irish whiskey for Piers and then, on impulse, went back for another one for Brian. Yes Brian; do not ask me why. I just did.

I had a nice flight back, but turbulence was very bad one hour out of JFK.

We had to abort the first landing attempt at JFK, and people were really scared.

The steward was sitting on the jump seat opposite me, and I asked him why we had to abort.

He said that he did not really know, "But there's nothing to worry about; we should be down in about fifteen minutes."

I wish they listened to their own comments sometimes. You do not tell a scared passenger that the plane will be down in fifteen minutes.

"Please rephrase what you said. 'We will *land* in about fifteen minutes' sounds much better; don't you think?"

He just smiled and said, "I guess you are right."

We did land in fifteen minutes; he came over and thanked me for flying with them, and he wished me well.

I guess he, too, had learned a lesson.

I had a few days off before I got back to work. I slept well that night, and the next day I dropped by Piers' apartment with the whiskey.

I rang the doorbell, and a young man opened the door. I asked if Piers was in and he said, "No, he is out, but I expect him back later."

"Please give this to him, and tell him Rose stopped by," I said, and I handed him the bottle of whiskey.

I went back up to my apartment, and thought Piers must have visitors for the holidays, and I thought no more about it.

I picked up Brian's card and dialed the number on it. A girl answered the phone and told me that he was not there, but he would be on duty later at 6:00 p.m. Did I want to leave a message for Doctor Kennedy? I left no message; I guess that was his office at the hospital.

I told her I would call back later, and I went about doing some laundry and other chores.

I called that number again at 6:15 p.m., and I got him.

"This is a surprise," he said.

I told him I was back in Ireland for Christmas, and I wanted to wish him a Happy New Year and I had brought him back a bottle of Irish whiskey, so I would like to meet him and give it to him.

"Let me get back to you... Oh! I don't have your number," he said.

I gave him my number, and he told me he would try to arrange a dinner with his parents at their house, and he would call me the next day.

Next day he did call and arranged to pick me up the following evening at 6:00 p.m. and take me to his parents' house.

"What is your address, Rose?" he asked.

I gave him all the directions, and told him I would see him tomorrow.

Now what have I done? What have I started?

I guess I am homesick, and I need an Irish voice to get me through it, and yes, his parents did invite me to dinner when I had met them at the restaurant.

Brian arrived at 6:00 p.m. on the dot, and we went about thirty minutes north of the city to his parents' house.

It was a very pretty Cape Cod, with beautiful gardens back and front.

I immediately felt comfortable with his parents, and we talked about Ireland and how much I missed it. His father Patrick was an electrician; he had his own small business, and his mother Kitty worked in a florist shop. I loved flowers, so we bonded immediately.

Patrick also reminded me of a cousin back home, same dry wit.

They both said, "Rose, come over anytime you like to visit and chat; we would love to hear more about our homeland too."

Dinner was shepherd's pie, a favorite of mine, and Brian was all talk at the dinner table.

His mother said, "We would love if he met up with a pretty Irish girl. Do you have a younger sister by any chance?"

Well, it hit me then that Brian was much younger, so I passed it off by asking her, "What age group are you looking at? I do have two younger sisters."

His mother said he had just qualified as a doctor and he worked in the ER at the local hospital. "He is just 27, and my only son, our only son."

You should have seen the look on the father's face before she corrected herself.

He was my sister's age, so I said, "I'll see what I can do."

In a way, I was relieved, as I did not want a romantic relationship at this time.

Brian's father Patrick was thrilled with the Irish whiskey, and asked me if I would like a drop.

I said, "No, I don't drink; it troubles my stomach."

"You are a sensible girl to stay away from that stuff; it would strip paint," said his mother Kitty.

"Have you seen a doctor about your tummy problems?" she asked.

I said, "Yes, and my doctor has me on medication, but I go back to her the end of this month for further tests."

"Well, if you need any further advice, Brian here will put you in touch with the right people. Won't you, Brian?" she said, as she nudged his arm.

"Sure Rose, we have great doctors at the hospital specializing in gastrointestinal disease, gastronomy, etc., so I will definitely put you on the right track," he said.

"I appreciate that very much," I said.

"Rose is a very pretty name," said his father. "Were you called after a relative?"

"No! Actually, I was christened Mary Rose, but Dad called me Rose from day one.

"He said Ireland was full of Mary(s). All my official papers have me as Mary.

"You should have been there when I went to Motor Vehicles to get my license.

"They insisted my name was Mary, even though I signed everything Rose. I got so frustrated I just gave up and said, 'Just put Mary R.,' so that's what is on my license."

Brian asked, "What's in the telephone directory?"

I said, "Nothing, it's ex-directory—why?"

"Just curious," he said. "You would make it very difficult for anyone to find you if you wanted to disappear." (*What a strange thing for him to say*, I thought.)

I found out much later that he had in fact tried to look me up in the telephone directory, but could not find my name. He had assumed it would be in the next addition of the directory.

The evening passed quickly, and I said, "I'd better head home; it's getting late."

Brian got up and said, "Okay, let's go before it's too late."

I thanked his parents, and his mother Kitty gave me their telephone number, and said, "Do call for a chat anytime, and do come again for dinner, and perhaps you will have found a nice Irish girl for Brian. I would hate to see him hitched to an American girl. They can be very selfish, and most of them are money grabbers."

I guess she can have her opinion, I thought to myself, and I promised her I would keep in touch, and Brian and I left.

We talked about Irish music and places to visit on his next trip over there, and before I knew, we were pulling into the curb at my apartment.

"I don't see a space to park, so will you be okay from here?" he asked.

"I'll be fine," I said. I thanked him for a lovely evening, and then I said, "I will keep in touch." "Please do, as I love your accent, and all the Irish stories you tell," he said.

As he left, he went on to say, "Perhaps you will find me an Irish girl; it's a pity I'm not ten years older— you would be my first choice you know, Rose."

I said, "Brian, why spoil a beautiful friendship," and we both laughed.

"I will wait here until you get inside," he said.

I walked quickly to the entrance, and I waved back to him, as I went inside.

My apartment was cold, so I turned up the heat and got ready for bed, and thought about what if I was ten years younger, and my thoughts went straight back to Kedrick.

I was awake most of the night, and kept thinking about Brian's comments, "It would be very difficult for anyone to find you."

Eventually I fell asleep, but when I awoke, I still had this on my mind.

I had Brian's mother's comments on my mind too— in no way did she want her doctor son to take up with an older woman, and she gave me that message straight away.

Well, Mrs. Irish Doctor's Mother, you need have no worries; this is purely nothing more than a friend-ship.

Nana's comments came to me then, "There is a reason for everything," and I asked myself the question, "What is the reason I became involved with this family?"

I felt so secure and relaxed with them—there had to be a reason.

I went shopping over the weekend to buy a dress for Pat and Ted's wedding, which was fast approaching. I had asked Pat what color and type she wanted me to wear, so I knew exactly what she wanted. I had already booked the flight.

The plan was to fly in two days before the wedding and stay with Brenda, and the day after the wedding,

I would drive down to see my parents and spend some time with them. I also wanted to visit Nana's grave.

I was to drive back to the city to catch the last flight back to New York on Sunday afternoon. I was due back at work on Monday morning.

Before all this, I had to return to see my doctor.

My doctor was always on time, and if you had an appointment for 5:30 p.m., you were seen at 5:30 p.m. I always made my appointments for the evenings; I had to pass her office on my way home from work, so it was very convenient. I decided to phone her first and I told her the medication was not working as well now, and she suggested I go have some tests done.

I said, "Okay, but I have to wait until after my friends' wedding on February 14th in Ireland."

"Sure, that's fine, Rose, but as soon as you get back, do drop in to my office and we will arrange all the tests for you. Keep taking the medication I have prescribed for you and have a safe trip." We said goodbye, and I hung up the phone.

AN IRISH WEDDING

If you have never been to an Irish wedding, then you have missed one of the greatest experiences in life; they can go on for days. Everybody gets dressed up, and hats are a big thing with the women. I love hats, so any excuse to wear one was very exciting for me.

I was so excited to meet Pat and Brenda, and all my other friends, and I had made up my mind to really enjoy myself. *Life is too short*, I thought.

Pat looked beautiful; the ceremony was just breathtaking and sentimental, and we did have the best time. We ate, danced, and drank until the early hours of the morning, and when we eventually got home, I just fell into bed, tired and exhausted, but very happy for Pat and Ted. Ted was being moved out to a suburban office, so Pat was thrilled about this. She felt more secure in the suburbs.

I felt terrible when I awoke, so I got up and got a glass of water and sipped it until Brenda appeared. She looked even worse than I did; her eyes were like two tadpoles in a chamber pot.

She insisted I have something for breakfast, as I had a long drive to my parents' house. It was a rental car, and I was not that familiar with it, and by now, I had gotten used to the fully automatic one.

I settled for some cornflakes and a banana, and soon I was on my way.

First, I had to drop by the assisted-living facility that Ellie was living in. She was so pleased to see me. I brought her a new nightdress, and we chatted for a few minutes before I had to leave. I did tell her I would keep in touch and hopefully come to see her again very soon.

My parents were thrilled to see me so soon again, even though it was only for a few hours. Dad and I went to the graveyard for a couple minutes. He said, "I guess it's the one thing in life we are sure about: we have to die someday." I made no comment because it scared me.

I loved coming home. My childhood home was large and comfortable, and the fridge was always full of healthy goodies, and some not too healthy, like cream cakes and fudge pies.

All the family looked fine. My younger sister Violet was still in college, and she still had no idea what she wanted to do. "Something in the pharmaceutical field maybe," she said.

My other sister Lily was very much settled into her career; she is a radiologist at our local hospital. My two brothers had taken up trades, and worked in my father's business.

Mam and Dad looked smaller, and then I thought, *That's my imagination—how can they look smaller?*

I found out they were both dieting, and I said, "For pity sakes, there is no need for you both to be dieting at this stage of your lives, just eat sensibly, and go for a walk each day."

They were not much overweight, maybe ten or fifteen pounds, and it is always better to carry a few pounds' excess, just in case you get sick, or so they say.

"Yes, but I'd rather carry the few pounds in my wallet," said Dad in his dry humorous way.

(I remember once when I did his books, before I went to Dublin, I noticed he was not billing people for his work. One case in particular, a local woman had her house burned down, and she had no insurance, so he built a new one for her, and never charged her anything. He was always giving money to his workers for home deposits, etc.).

I said, "Dad, you need to stop this as you will need it in your retirement," and do you know what his reply was? "Have you ever seen a hearse with a U-Haul behind it? I can't take it with me."

I dropped the conversation then, as I did now, and I went on to something else.

I asked Mam to make out a list of things she would like me to bring back to her when I returned home in twelve months.

"Think about it, and you can mail it to me," I said.

Soon, it was time to head back as I did not want to be tied up in traffic, and miss my flight.

My sister Lily shouted to me, "Rose, I will come visit you when I get my holidays."

"Good Lily, do that, and we can go shopping," I said.

I waved goodbye, and I was on my way. My flight was uneventful, not like the last one, and I got home safe, but I was very tired.

The break did pick me up, and when I got to the office the next morning, I was full of energy.

Jerry called me in to his office and asked if I would go to Germany with him in two weeks; it was to Cologne, and he needed someone with a financial background at the meetings.

"Sure, hopefully I will have recovered from the wedding by then," I said.

That evening I called Piers, and he said he had some kind of flu or other, so he said I was to stay clear of him, as he did not want to pass it along to me.

I told him I was going to Cologne in two weeks and he said, "We will have dinner when you get back; I should be better by then, and hopefully I will be back on my feet."

I had been to Cologne several times before, so I knew how to get around the city, and I always visited the cathedral there and rubbed my hand on the doorknob. They say if you do that, you will return, so I was looking forward to this trip very much. I also bought their famous cologne, and I took it home to my Mam each time I visited; she loved it.

I called my doctor and told her I had to travel again, and I would contact her as soon as I got back.

"Rose, please don't put it on the long finger," she said.

"I promise, Doctor. I'll come in as soon as I get back," I told her.

I called Brian's mother Kitty and told her all about the wedding. I said I would be traveling to Cologne in two weeks and I would contact her as soon as I got back, and to give my regards to her husband Patrick and to Brian.

"I am still looking for that nice Irish gal for him," I said.

Don't ask me why I said that. I guess I was reassuring her I had no romantic feelings for her doctor son, or was I just getting my dig in? Who knows, I thought, and I went to run a nice hot bath for myself, and I turned on the radio.

I put in my favorite bath oil, and settled down for a relaxing bath, with soothing music in the background.

As I lay there, I began to look back over the years, and wondered what the future held for me.

I also reminded myself that my biological clock was ticking. I would like to have children before I was too old, but I was not getting married for the wrong reasons.

I got out and wrapped myself in a large towel, and sat at my dresser mirror, just staring at myself.

"Rose, you are a very lucky girl," I said aloud.

I had found and loved my soul mate, and he did return that love; some people go through life and never experience those feelings.

He had said I was "his perfect Rose."

I wiped the tears from my cheeks, got ready for bed, and went to turn off the radio when our song, "Strangers in the Night," came on.

I just sat on the side of my bed, closed my eyes, and listened. *He can hear me*, I thought. I climbed into bed, and I had a very peaceful night's sleep.

Kedrick is here with me; I just know it.

Next day I asked Jerry at the office if he had made up the schedule for our trip and he said, "Sit down, and we will do it now, Rose."

We made out a list of meetings that he needed to have, and we set aside time for two dinners to entertain the clients.

"I will contact them today to verify that this fits their schedule," he said.

I asked if I could be excused from at least one dinner, as I would like to meet my friend Karen and have some time with her.

"I don't see why not. I really only need you to be there at the meetings," he said.

"Good, I will contact her and see if she is free on either of those nights," and I got up to go back to my office, and I put in a call to Karen.

Karen was the accounting manager with an airline company in Cologne. I had met her years ago; we became friends, and we have kept in touch over the years.

She was the one that took me to the cathedral and told me the story about the doorknob.

We set up a meeting place, and I went back to my work.

I was so looking forward to this trip and meeting Karen again.

THE COLOGNE TRIP

It was a wonderful trip, very good businesswise, and I so enjoyed meeting Karen, and we did get to the cathedral, and I said a prayer for you know who, and I put my hand on the doorknob, and I promised her I would come back again, very soon.

Jerry was a real nice traveling companion; it was my first trip with him, and he was witty and chatty and helped me with my baggage, so I felt real good as the taxi dropped me back to my apartment.

"Life is good," I said.

I thought, *Maybe I can dream again.* Now if only my stomach felt as good and I put a note on my calendar to call my doctor before the week was over.

I showered and got to bed early, as the jet lag was getting to me recently.

It's no fun getting up there in years; the big four-o was just a few years away, but then again, they say, "Life begins at forty." We shall see, I said to myself, but I still had a few years to go.

I called Piers during the week to say I was back, and to see if he was over his flu, and did he want to go to dinner.

He said, "Rose, can we postpone dinner until next week? I am still awaiting test results," and he went on to ask about my trip, and what the weather was like in Cologne, and where did I stay, etc., so I said, "I hope you feel better real soon, Piers, and I'll call you next week," and I put the phone down.

Something is not quite right with him; perhaps I should go down to his apartment to see for myself, but I had second thoughts, and I decided to leave it until next week.

Strange, he never mentioned the bottle of whisky, and who was that young man that answered his door? Again, "Curious Rose" took over, and I decided to check it all out next week.

I finally made that appointment with my doctor, and she said she was sending me for tests: a colonoscopy and an endoscopy. "I just want to make sure everything is okay. Have to consider your family history of stomach problems, including cancer."

The tests were scheduled for the following week at a specialist's office.

His office was in the medical building attached to the hospital. I went to see him the day before the tests, and he wanted to do two separate tests.

I said, "Why?"

He said to me while shaking his head, "Insurance has a problem paying for two tests at a time."

Who runs those companies? I wondered to myself. Common sense says it is cheaper to have both done at the same time, but I guess they have their reasons.

I said to him, "You are only getting me under once, so do what you have to do then. I'll handle the insurance if there is a problem."

He was great, and he said, "Rose, if that's what you want, that's fine," so all was arranged for the next day.

My assistant, Beth from the office, was coming with me. I had become very good friends with Beth. It was just in and out, same day, and I was taking a few days off work afterwards. Jerry had insisted, so that I would be fit for some important meetings the following week.

I called Brian's mother Kitty, and told her about my tests, and she said, "I'll have Brian call you when he gets home. He probably knows the doctor that is doing them."

I had just gotten into bed at around 9:30 p.m. when the phone rang. It was Brian.

I told him what I was having done and he said, "He is a very good doctor, and very thorough in following up with his patients. I'll call you tomorrow evening to see how it went, or would you like me to take you?" He told me he was not on duty in the morning.

I said, "Thanks Brian, but Beth is taking me; she is picking me up at 8:00 a.m., so it's all arranged."

"Who is Beth?" He asked.

"My assistant from the office," I told him.

"Okay, I will call you later; have a good night's sleep, and don't worry about anything. All will be fine," he said and hung up.

Beth was a treasure; she was African-American, and she was very pretty.

I had never worked with any black person before. I found out she was just like me underneath; she had the same desires to succeed in life, and her family was very important to her. We may have a different colored skin, but we were really the same. My parents brought me up to treat everyone as an equal. It's really fear of the unknown; that is what can cause problems sometimes, so communication is very important in life.

I remembered I had not told Piers, as the last time I phoned him, there was no reply, and his answering machine did not pick up. I guessed he was away. I will call him on my days off, and I pulled the sheets around my neck and soon was fast asleep.

THE TESTS

Beth arrived bright and early, and as I was fasting, I just lay in bed until the last minute.

I had a quick shower, and dressed in sweats to be more comfortable.

The procedure took about one hour, but we were there until noon before they eventually let me go home. The nurse came over to us and said, "The doctor will contact your doctor tomorrow, so she should call you with the results. She should have them around noon," and she asked me if I was feeling okay. I thanked her, and we headed home.

I was a little lightheaded and sleepy, but otherwise I was fine.

Beth asked if I wanted anything to eat and I said, "No, I'll just make some tea later, for now I will just lie down on the couch and rest."

"Well, call me if you need anything as I have to get back to the office," she said, and she left.

I felt a bit queasy, but I was fine just lying there, and of course, the mind starts thinking, and all of a sudden, I sat up and shouted aloud to myself, "I have no picture of him."

Kedrick and I never had a picture taken together in all our travels. We never had a camera with us. I never gave him a picture of myself, and he never gave me one. Maybe this was deliberate on his part; remember, he was still legally married.

The only thing I had belonging to him was a white turtleneck cotton tee with his name inside on a nametag. I had asked him for it so that I could sleep with it when we were apart for any length of time.

I had remembered Tim's friend Karl from West Germany, and him taking a picture from his wallet of his fiancée Ria. (I hope he got her across the wall.)

I really did not need a picture of Kedrick; he was as clear in my mind today as the day I first met him, and of course, I had so many dreams of him.

I must have dozed off to sleep, and the phone's ringing woke me up. It was Beth saying she was leaving the office, "Are you okay? Do you need anything?"

"I'm fine, thank you," I answered in a half-awake half-asleep voice.

"Okay, I will call you tomorrow; sleep well tonight," she said and she hung up.

I went into the kitchen to fix something light to eat, and when the phone rang again, it was Brian.

He asked how my tests went, and I told him I had to contact my doctor after noon tomorrow and she should have the results.

"Okay, I will call you again tomorrow night. I am working until 9:00 p.m., so try to get a good sleep tonight, and I'll talk to you tomorrow," he said, and

I wished him a good night, and I hung up the phone and went on preparing my snack.

Next morning I felt better, and I tried to call Piers, but again no answer. *He must be away*, I thought. A short time later, I got anxious about him; he usually tells me when he is going away.

I decided to walk down to his apartment on the second floor.

His door was ajar and I shouted, "Are you in there, Piers?"

A woman with a mop in her hand came to the door, and said she was his cleaning lady.

I told her who I was, and asked her if she knew where he was.

"Oh! He had mentioned if you called I was to tell you he had taken a sudden flight to some clinic in Paris to have some more tests done, and that he will be back in a few days, and he will call you as soon as he gets back." She was nearly out of breath when she finished.

"Is he okay?" I asked her.

"Well, he hasn't said anything to me, but I can tell he is worried about something.

"I have cleaned for him for over ten years, so I can tell something is not right," and then she blessed herself and said, "I hope he will be fine."

I thanked her and went back to my apartment, as I had to call my doctor.

Deep down, I was very worried about Piers; something is seriously wrong with him, I kept thinking to myself. I guess I would have to wait until I heard from him.

I picked up the phone and called my doctor.

"Rose, I need you to come into my office at 10:00 a.m. in the morning; we have to discuss your test results," she said. "I got all your results back."

"Is it bad news?" I asked.

"No, we just need to discuss the test results, and see if we need any further ones.

"I'll see you in the morning, and don't go worrying about anything," and she put her phone down.

I was still holding mine five minutes later, just listening to the buzz and convinced that something was wrong.

What do I do now? Do I call someone? Do I call my parents? I decided to do nothing until I saw her in the morning and got all the facts.

I took the phone off the hook and tried to get some sleep, but it was just a few minutes at a time, so I got up early and tried to eat breakfast, and I suddenly remembered that Brian was to call me last night. "I will tell him tonight when I have more details," I said to myself.

I got to the doctor's office very early, a half hour before my appointment.

She took me in as soon as she saw me in the waiting room.

She told me that she wanted to do some extra tests, and she went on to tell me that my colonoscopy was fine, but I did have a large "mass" in my stomach.

"This needs a biopsy, and I need you to have it done within a few days. As soon as we get those results back, then we will take it from there." She was not really looking at me; she kept looking at the test results.

"Is it cancer?" I asked.

"We don't think so; that's why we need a biopsy to make sure," she said.

I decided not to tell my parents until I had the biopsy, so I called Jerry at the office and I told him, and he told me to take all the time I needed and, "I'll have Beth take you in like last time. I assume it's just in and out, same day, or are they keeping you overnight?" He asked.

"I haven't got the appointment yet, but my doctor tells me it only takes a few minutes to take the biopsy. I will probably be there a few hours, but I expect to be let home that day," I said.

"Well, if you need anything, call me, and things will be fine, so don't worry until you have to, which I hope is never. Try to get some rest and take care," he said and he hung up.

My doctor was to ring me next day to let me know if she had set up the biopsy.

Again, it was another restless night, and a real calm came over me, and I thought, *Well, if it is bad news, perhaps this is the way I will finally find Kedrick again.*

I know he will be waiting for me when I cross over, and I fell asleep with those thoughts.

The doctor called next day to say my biopsy was scheduled for the following week, Wednesday, at the same medical center, but with another doctor.

I asked, "Why another doctor?"

She replied, "This one specializes in gastrointestinal problems, and he is very highly respected."

I just sat around all day and Brian phoned, and I told him what had happened.

He said, "Rose, you are in good hands, and if you need a surgeon, I know just the person. He is South African, and he is the best there is in his field."

We chatted for a while and he said, "Rose, why not come over to my parents on Sunday? We can have my mother's Sunday roast, and I am off that day too. Well, what do you say?" he said.

"I'd love that," I said.

"Fine, I will call her and tell her, and I will call you back with the time that I will collect you, and in the meantime, don't worry. All will be fine." He said.

I said, "Thanks Brian. I really appreciate this. I could do with some friendly Irish company," and I hung up.

I called Beth and told her my appointment was for Wednesday, but I told her I would drop in to the office for a few hours on Monday and Tuesday, and attend those meetings Jerry had set up. "I'll talk to you then," I told her.

"Rose, I'll be here if you need me, and have a great weekend," she said, and we both hung up our phones at the same time.

Brian called back to say he would pick me up at 3:00 p.m. on Sunday, so I went to the local store and picked up some food for myself, and a bottle of wine to take with me on Sunday to his parents' house.

I still had not heard from Piers, so I was worried, but there was nothing I could do until I heard from him. It seemed like déjà vu all over again.

Sunday, 3:00 p.m., and Brian was there to pick me up. *Always on time*, I thought.

He seems to be a very reliable person. Well, he is a doctor, so I guess it is in his nature.

We chatted as we drove to his home, and I asked if he still lived there full time.

He went on to tell me that he had large student loans to repay, so he still lived at home for the moment anyway, and it suited his parents too to have him around.

"I have my own room at the hospital if I need some space, so for now, it's fine," he said.

"Of course, if you find me that nice Irish girl, I will have to move out," and he looked at me rather sheepishly. We both laughed.

We had a lovely Sunday roast. I stayed until 7:00 p.m., just chatting and talking, and his mother Kitty said if I needed her, she would come with me to the hospital.

I thanked her and said, "I'll keep that in mind, but Beth from the office is taking me."

We said goodnight to his parents, and Brian drove me home.

"I'll call you later in the week, and see if you have any results; sometimes biopsies can take time for results to come back," he said.

He waited by the curb until I got to the door of the building. I waved back to him and he drove off.

I had just taken off my shoes and was putting the kettle on when the phone rang.

It was Piers. I said, "Where are you?"

"On my way up to see you, if that is okay," he said.

"Good, I have just put the kettle on, so you can join me for a cup of tea, good Irish tea," I said.

"I'll be right up, Rose," he said.

He looked weary when he came in, and I asked him if he was all right.

"Well, I feel I owe you an apology for keeping you in the dark, but I wanted to be sure first before I told anyone," he replied with a big sigh.

He told me he had not been feeling well recently, and he thought it was the flu.

"All the blood work was coming back abnormal, so I have had test after test, and no one was coming up with an answer. They kept saying it was something to do with my kidneys.

"Finally, I went to see a specialist, and I do have serious kidney problems.

"He thinks I may need a kidney transplant. My cousin is a kidney specialist in a clinic in Paris, so I called him, and he had me fly over at once. Well, to cut a long story short, things are not as bad as they seemed. One kidney may have to go, but the other should be fine after treatment.

"I was so scared, Rose!" he said, and he took my hand and held it.

"I kept thinking I had this strange disease called AIDS, but thank God it's definitely not that," he said.

"Why did you think you had AIDS, Piers?" I asked.

"Well, I had surgery a few years ago for prostrate problems, and I had several pints of blood afterwards, and now they are saying that tainted blood can cause AIDS.

"You have no idea how scared I was, Rose," and he actually had tears in his eyes as he spoke.

I said, "Let's have that cup of tea. I have some apple pie too—would you like some?"

"I'd love it," he replied.

"By the way, Piers, did you ever get that bottle of Irish whiskey I left for you?"

"So that's where it came from," he replied.

I went on to tell him I had given it to a young man that answered the door to his apartment.

"My nephew Jody was staying with me for New Year's. He wanted to be in Times Square for the celebrations. He wanted to see Dick Clark up close and in person, and he just put it in my drink cabinet and never told me. I just found it a few days ago," he said.

Another mystery solved, I said to myself, and a lesson learned—never jump to conclusions, always wait for the full story, and we sat down to enjoy our tea.

I decided to wait until we were finished before I told him my story.

"So what's next for you now?" I asked him.

"Well, my cousin is contacting the specialist here, and they will work out what form of treatment I need, and we will take it from there," he sounded relieved as he spoke.

"I have some news of my own, Piers. I go in for a biopsy on Wednesday," and I told him all about my tests. "I haven't told my family yet, as I want the biopsy results first, and then as you said, just take it from there. I don't want to worry them unless I have to."

"I guess we both have been holding out on each other," he said. "Rose, you know I am here for you if you need me," and again he held my hand.

"I consider you one of my best friends, Piers," I said.

"Thank you, Rose; you mean the world to me too, and we will both get through this difficult time together, just by being there for each other."

He gave me a big hug and then said, "By the way, who was that good-looking guy that just dropped you off? Is it someone from work?"

"No, actually it's a long story, but he is Irish, and I have become friends with his family.

"He is a doctor in the ER at the local hospital, and he has been very helpful to me recently."

I went on to tell him how we met, and that I had dinner with his parents that evening.

"He is much younger than me, and his mother Kitty has made it very clear that I am too old for him, and you do not mess with Irish mothers and their sons.

"I am glad to have them as friends too. I consider myself lucky to be surrounded by a great group of friends, especially being so far away from my family."

He gave me another hug and said, "Rose, you are a special person, and I'm very proud to have you as my friend. I feel blessed to know you."

We finished our tea, and he left, telling me to keep him in the picture.

"You too," I said, and I started to get ready for bed.

I was going into work in the morning for a few hours to attend a meeting.

I had strange dreams all night—people I did not know, places I had never been to. However, one woman, a tall blonde-haired woman, kept reappearing everyplace I would go in my dreams.

I awoke, and I was very confused as to what this meant, if anything at all.

I guess it was all those tests that I had been through; they must have screwed up my mind.

Finally, it was time to get up and shower and dress for work.

Jerry had arranged to pick me up; he did not want me taking the subway in case I picked up some germ or other before my biopsy.

I was so glad to have gone to the office; we were very busy, and it kept my mind off Wednesday and my biopsy.

"I will come in again tomorrow," I told him. "It makes me feel better, and it keeps my mind occupied, no time for self-pity."

"Fine, if that's what you want and I'll pick you up again, and Beth or someone will drop you home; now let's get you home today," he said.

Both Brian and Piers telephoned to see how I was doing on Tuesday night, and they said they would call again later in the week. If I needed anything, I was to call them.

Brian even gave me his pager number in case I needed reassurance.

I decided to give my sister Lily a call to let her know what was going on, but I asked her to keep silent about it until I got the biopsy results. It was very late, but she was still up and she wanted to fly over straight away, but I said, "No need for that, wait until I get the results, and then if I need surgery, you can come over for a few weeks."

I told her I would call her as soon as I got the results.

"Please don't mention anything to Mam or Dad; I don't want them worrying too," I said.

"Okay then, but call me as soon as you get your results," she said.

I was just getting ready for bed, when the phone rang. It was Bill from Boston.

His mother Betty had passed away. I explained I was unable to attend the funeral as I was having medical tests done. He understood, and told me to keep in touch. I asked him for the funeral information so that I could send some flowers. I immediately rang the flower people; thankfully, they were open twenty-four/seven. I sent a real nice wreath, with a sympathy note attached. I would write a letter to Sally when I was back in action again.

I had another restless night. I guess deep down I was worried. Well, I had the tests and Betty's death on my mind, and eventually I fell asleep with Kedrick's tee under my pillow. Yes, I still had it after all those years. Somehow, it made me feel secure.

Beth was on time as usual, and we got to the medical center with time on our hands. I told her to go get a coffee for herself while the nurse was putting the IV in my hand.

I hate those things. I have small veins and I usually have problems, but thankfully, it was fine this time.

I don't remember anything after that until I woke up, and the nurse was telling me, "Rose, it's all over," and I heard her say, "When you feel able, press this button and I will come and help you to dress. Your friend is here to take you home."

Before I left the building, I was advised to contact my doctor in a few days, probably two to three days, and she should have the results.

Beth dropped me off, as all I wanted to do was crawl into bed. She waited until I got inside.

I slept for a few hours, and then called my sister Lily to say I was home.

I told her, "I may have the results before the weekend, so I will call you then, but in the meantime, say nothing to anyone until I get the results. I don't want anyone worrying just yet."

I put a robe on, and turned on the radio, and I went to make some tea and toast.

It must have been Elvis hour, because all his songs were being played. I loved Elvis; I grew up with his music. His music is timeless; it will never go out of fashion.

The phone never stopped ringing for the next few hours—Brian, Piers, Brian's mother Kitty, and of course several from the office. It is so nice to know that people care, especially when your own family is so far away. *There are good people in this crazy world of ours,* I thought.

I felt much better the next day, and I decided to go into the office for a few hours.

The "Trade Embargo" had done some damage to our monthly sales, but we had made gains in other areas, so it was not a complete disaster. Only time will tell what the long-term outlook will be and if we can keep the NY office open. I hope so.

I kept busy, but I left before the rush hour, saying, "And I'll see you all in the morning."

I ran a bath when I got home, and I just lay there listening to the radio, when I heard our song, "Strangers in the Night," come on. This time it had a very calming effect on me. *Kedrick is sending me a message,* I thought to myself.

I had a lazy evening and ate a light meal, and headed to bed around 9:30 p.m.

Again, I had strange dreams, and that woman was in one of them. I was on a boat with her, but I could not see her face, and I had no idea where we were going. *All so strange*, I thought, when I awoke.

Well, for one thing, no one is ever getting me on a boat again, so I put it out of my mind (or tried to).

We had another busy day at the office, and I stayed later than I had intended to.

My phone rang, as I was just about to leave the office; it was my doctor.

I was just frozen stiff for a second until I heard, "Rose, it's good news. It's benign; however, I need you to come into the office next week to discuss treatment, and where we go from here," she said.

I could tell, by her voice, she was very relieved.

"Thank you, Doctor. I'll call you Monday to set up an appointment," I said.

I do not even remember the ride home. I was so relieved, and I called my sister Lily straight away. She was more excited than I was, and said she was coming over in a few weeks anyway for her holidays.

"You can tell them the news at home, and I'll call you after I've seen my doctor next week," and we chatted for a few more minutes and I said, "Have a good night," and I rang off.

It was Friday evening, and I decided to call Piers to tell him, and perhaps we could go out to eat Saturday evening. Piers was thrilled with the news, and we did arrange to have dinner the next evening. He told me he was also feeling much better. I guess it was peace of mind more than anything else with him, actually for both of us.

I called Brian's mother Kitty (I could not get Brian), and she kept saying, "Thank God, Rose. I will tell Brian when he comes in."

I just could not get her off the phone; she went on, and on, and finally I had to tell her that I had to go, and I would talk to her next week.

I had a real nice relaxing night; I watched a movie and went to bed around 11:00 p.m.

I slept soundly, and felt so refreshed and real good when I awoke.

I had a small leisurely breakfast, made some phone calls overseas, and dressed to go food shopping locally.

The doorbell rang, as I was just about to go out. I checked out who was there, and I saw a florist lady standing there with a large basket of fruit. I opened my door, took them in, and read the card that was enclosed. It was from Kitty, Patrick, and Brian.

How thoughtful of them, and I made a mental note to ring them to thank them when I got back from shopping.

I did not buy much, so I walked slowly with my bags back to the apartment.

VIOLATION OF PRIVACY

The door to my apartment was ajar, and I panicked, had I gone out and left it open?

Then I saw a piece of wood; it was lying on the floor. The door had been busted in.

I dropped my bags, and I ran to Piers' apartment. Luckily, he was there, so I told him what I had seen, and he immediately called the police.

They told him not to let me back into the apartment until they got here, as the intruder could still be there. It was much later before I was permitted to go back into my apartment.

Piers had taken my shopping bags down to his apartment, so I went in to check and see what was taken. A police officer and Piers came with me.

What a mess—drawers pulled out, underwear all over the floor, and jewelry boxes strewn all over the place, all empty. I noticed that my basket of fruit had been pulled open and was strewn all over the place; I think some was missing.

I just started to cry, and Piers held me, "Rose, it's just material stuff; thankfully, you were not here and you did not get hurt. Things can be replaced, but you can't," he said, while he was still holding me in his arms.

The detective asked me to make up a list of the items that were missing and to drop it off at the local station when I had it ready. I told him I would do that in a day or so.

They had dusted for fingerprints. Piers called someone to come fix my door, and he requested an additional lock be fitted to the door.

We tidied up the place. I got my shopping from Piers' apartment, and we waited for the repairperson to come. When all was back in order, it was quite late, so Piers said, "Just get changed, and we will go to dinner and forget all about this, and you can sleep in my spare room tonight. I don't want you on your own, and tomorrow, you can go through what's missing."

Dinner was nice, but my mind was elsewhere, so I told him I would be fine in my own apartment, and I would ring him if I needed him.

"Are you sure, Rose?" he asked.

"Yes, I'll be fine," I said.

I double-bolted my apartment door, and I went into my bedroom to make a start on the list for the detective. I know it was very late, but I needed to get a start on it.

All my gold jewelry was gone, including my grandmother's wedding and engagement rings, my late aunt's engagement ring, and then I realized that the pin Kedrick had given me was on the lapel of a jacket. I ran to the closet to check if it was there, and yes, it was still there.

It was the one thing that had survived; everything else of value was gone. I remembered another of Nana's sayings: "May all the bad luck go with them."

I really was not too upset now, because I had that one special pin, my emerald and diamond ladybug, and at this moment, this is all I needed.

I did not sleep much that night. I just kept tossing and turning, and hearing noises all night.

Maybe I should have slept at Piers' place, I thought, and I was glad when it was time to get up.

I had just finished breakfast when Brian phoned.

"I heard the good news, and as I mentioned, if you do need surgery, and I think you may, there is only one surgeon that should do it.

"It is a Doctor Gary Clerken from Johannesburg. He is the best. Actually, his wife is a doctor also, and they work as a team. Both are attached to a city hospital, but they also have their own practice.

"When do you go back to your doctor?" he asked.

"Well, I have to ring her on Monday to schedule the appointment, so I'll let you know and I'll also tell her about your suggestions, if she thinks I need surgery.

"Oh, by the way, my sister Lily is coming to visit in a few weeks—would you like to meet her?" I asked.

"I'd love to," he said, and we chatted a little longer, and I told him all about my burglary, and how all my jewelry was taken, etc., and he was so nice and caring, and said, "It's only material things, Rose." I told him that's what Piers had said too.

"Sorry Rose, but I have to go as I am on duty today. I'll talk to you later in the week, and Rose, chin up; you are a survivor," and he rang off.

I forgot to thank him for the fruit basket. I will call Kitty later to thank her; I guess she was the one that sent it anyway, because she works in a florist shop.

I spent the day sorting out my clothes, and decided to throw out all my underwear.

It was the most awful feeling knowing someone had handled then and thrown them on the floor, and probably walked all over them, and who knows what else they had done to them.

I called my insurance company to report the loss, and guess what: I was not covered for my jewelry. I did not have a rider on my policy for the jewelry. No one had ever mentioned that I needed one. Live and learn. It was a costly lesson, but then, as the men said, "It's only material things and they can be replaced."

I went shopping in the afternoon and stocked up on new items; it felt good getting all new items. I went to bed that night and slept soundly, no dreams.

My appointment was scheduled for Wednesday evening after work, so I busied myself at work all day, and I called into my doctor's office on the way home.

I was a little nervous, as I did not know what she was going to recommend.

MAJOR DECISIONS

My doctor told me the mass in my stomach was growing, and down the road, it could cause a blockage, and then it could possibly become an emergency, and this could be very dangerous.

Her recommendation was surgery now, rather than later in life.

I was in very good health now, and who knows, I may not be as fit later in life.

I told her about Doctor Clerken that Brian had recommended, and she said, "Yes, a very good choice. It is difficult getting an appointment with him, but I worked with him on a special case last year, so I will put in a call and see if I can get you a consultation.

"He *is* the best. He came here several years ago with his wife, who is also a doctor; they have their own practice. She is also a great surgeon and specializes in children's cases, but she assists and fills in for him sometimes."

We talked a little longer, and she said, "I'll call you with your appointment date; hopefully, it will be sooner rather than later."

I thanked her, and I left her office and I started to walk home.

I needed some fresh air, and I wanted to clear my mind.

I was glad when Friday came around. Friday 6:00 p.m. was my favorite time; work was finished for the week, and I had the weekend to do whatever I wanted to do.

By 6:00 p.m. I was home. I kicked off my shoes, loosened my bra, and I was ready to relax.

I decided over the weekend to go ahead with the surgery; my doctor was right—get it done now while in good health.

I decided to go to Chicago to see my cousins. I would fly in on a Friday evening and back on a late flight Sunday, the following weekend. I felt I needed to be with family at this time.

They were my father's nieces and nephews, and we were close in age.

It was a great reunion. We got very little sleep, just sitting up late and catching up on past and present memories. Family is so important in this life; it makes the journey that much easier.

I got back late Sunday, and my doctor had left a message on my answering machine to contact her office on Monday morning early, as she had managed to get a consultation with the surgeon for me on Friday at 3:00 p.m. She needed to give me all the paperwork to bring to him, for him to review.

He was to review it, and then he would consult her, and me, on the next step.

Friday afternoon came quickly, and as I sat nervously in the waiting room, waiting for my name to be called, I tried to remain calm.

The room had pictures and posters of South Africa all over the place.

Plaques lined one wall with credentials, and it was very tastefully decorated.

Just as I had started to look at the plaques, a very pretty nurse came out and called my name.

I got up to follow her, and she showed me into a room with a couch, and a desk and chairs, all beautifully coordinated.

South African posters and pictures also decorated this room. One wall was lined with books, and a large plant was on one side. It just made you feel so relaxed.

I even had the feeling that I was here before, but I knew that this was not possible.

She pointed to a chair and said, "Please take a seat, Rose. Doctor Clerken will be with you in a few minutes."

The doctor came in and shook my hand, and he went to sit behind his desk.

"Well, Rose Kelly, let me see what I can do for you," and he looked straight into my eyes.

He opened the envelope with all the documentation, and he spent several minutes reading the reports and looking at the films from the endoscopy.

He was talking to me as he was reading the reports. "Biopsies only take samples from the surface, and this is a very large mass, so my recommendation is to have it removed. It is in the lining of the stomach, so I will have to remove a small part of your stomach also."

He went on to tell me what the procedure would entail. "The surgery takes between three to five hours, and your expected stay in the hospital is about six or seven days...

"Where is your accent from?" He asked.

"Ireland," I replied.

"I went golfing there last year, and I can't wait to go back. I loved it. They have wonderful clinics there also, very up to date with equipment and treatments."

He continued to talk to me a few minutes more, and by the time I left, I was completely at ease and had 100% confidence in him.

He said he would call my doctor that day, and he would tell her what we had decided on.

His nurse would contact me with all the details, and schedule a date for surgery, probably in three to four weeks.

I thanked him and left his office, and I went back through the waiting room.

I saw a woman down the hallway, and I thought she looked very familiar, tall and blonde.

It was just a fleeting glance, and I could not see her face properly, yet I felt I had seen her somewhere before. Maybe she was like someone I had met on my travels, who knows, I thought to myself, but it was strange.

I called my sister Lily when I got home, and I told her the news.

She said she would come over for a few weeks until I got back on my feet.

She had a month's vacation, and she could take a few weeks leave of absence as well, so she would be here for nearly two months.

"Hopefully, you will be back at work by then," she said.

I told her, "I have a very nice young doctor all lined up for you, so you will not be bored."

We laughed, and chatted a little longer, and I told her as soon as I got the actual date I would let her know, so that she could book her flight.

THE SURGERY

Doctor Clerken's nurse called the following week, saying that my surgery was scheduled for three weeks later, on a Wednesday. She would mail me all the details, on where to go for my pre-op tests and my blood work, etc.

My sister Lily booked her flight for the weekend before, so that she would be familiar with the area and how to get to the hospital—all this, before I went in for the surgery.

Now it was just waiting. I kept busy at work and at home, anything to occupy my mind.

I was not scared at all. I had a very good feeling about my surgeon, and I was prepared to place myself 100% in his hands. He was also from South Africa and this meant a lot, but it also rekindled some memories, memories that were still very clear in my mind, even after all those years.

Lily arrived on the Saturday before my surgery, and I met her at the airport. We drove straight to my apartment.

It was her first time in New York, and she was not impressed with the traffic jams and how untidy the city was. After she had rested, I showed her around my apartment. She did like it, and said, "It is just beautiful, and you were so lucky to find it."

"Actually Piers found it for me," I replied. I told her about Piers and that he lived downstairs.

Next day I showed her how to operate all the appliances and where all the plugs were.

I gave her Piers' telephone number and his apartment number, just in case she needed anything. He was to drop by later anyway.

I was also trying to get Brian to drop by before I went in on Wednesday, but I could not get hold of him. I left a message for him to contact me.

We spent a quiet weekend, and Piers phoned to say he would drop by later on Sunday evening.

I had to go for my pre-op tests on Monday, so I finished up at work on Friday, and I told them I would probably be out for two months.

Jerry told me to take as long as I needed, saying, "Remember Rose, your health is the first priority right now," and he gave me a big hug as I left.

I went to the bank on Friday and took out some extra cash, just in case Lily needed anything for the apartment. So I was all set for Wednesday; I had all my affairs in order.

I realized it was major surgery, but I was very calm and relaxed about the whole thing.

I felt I was in very good hands.

Piers dropped by Sunday evening as promised, and he spent some time with us.

He told Lily to call him if she needed anything.

After he left, Lily said, "Rose, he is cute! What's the story there?"

I told her, "We have been friends for years, and I just found out he had major prostrate surgery a few years ago, so I'm guessing that's why he doesn't get serious with any girl. I may be wrong, but it rather adds up to what I know about him.

"He is a real friend, with no strings attached, and this suits me. ...I still haven't gotten over Kedrick."

"Rose," she yelled at me, "for God's sake, it's been what ten, twelve years?"

"Yes, yes Lily, I know, and as soon as I am back in Ireland next spring, I am going to Cape Town to finalize things once and for all." I gave a big sigh and then went on to say, "Perhaps you will come with me?"

"Well if that's what it takes, sure, I'll go with you," she said. "You have a life to live, Rose; please put the past behind you—it's time. Keep the memories but get on with life."

On our way back from my pre-op tests on Monday I showed her where the local stores were, and when we got back to my apartment, I made a pot of tea, and we were just sitting down to drink it when the phone rang. It was Brian.

"Sorry, sorry... I had to work back-to-back shifts, but I will drop by later," he said.

"That is fine, and you can meet my sister Lily then," I told him.

"What time can we expect you?" I asked.

"I'll be there before 7:00 p.m.; can I bring anything?" he asked.

"No. Thanks anyway, we are fine, and I will have something ready for you to eat, something light," I said.

"See you later," he said and rang off.

Brian arrived just before 7:00 p.m. as he had promised, and he looked exhausted.

I could tell right away he was impressed with Lily, and she with him.

I had made a salad, so we all sat down to eat it with a glass of wine. (*Probably my last for a while*, I thought.)

We chatted and laughed, and before we knew, it was midnight.

"Oh my goodness, I'm so sorry to have kept you both up so late. I better go," he said.

I asked him to keep an eye on Lily while I was in the hospital, and he said, "I'd be delighted, and I will pop in and see you too, Rose. What time is surgery scheduled for?"

I told him, "11:30 a.m.—make sure to get your friends there to take good care of me, and do not forget to show Lily around." I said goodnight to him, and I let Lily show him to the door.

She came back about fifteen minutes later, looking blushed, and said, "He is nice, actually very nice."

She had a grin from ear to ear on her face as she said this.

"He gave me his phone number to call him if I needed anything, but he said he would get in touch with me. It could be an interesting trip," and she laughed and said, "Let's get some sleep, Rose, as you will need it." We both slept soundly.

Next day, Piers called to say he would drop us both to the hospital on Wednesday morning. Lily was to call him when it was all over, and he would come pick her up and take her home. Everything was organized before I left for my surgery. I was an organizer; I liked to have all my "I's" dotted and my "T's" crossed.

The hospital was very crowded and extremely busy that morning. I was shown into a cubicle, and an IV was inserted in my hand. Lily was allowed to sit with me during this time.

The anesthetist came by and asked many questions. (I guess they need to know everything about you; after all, you are putting your life in their hands.)

The nurse came to take me to the operating room. I was to walk there.

I remembered an old saying: "If you walk into a hospital, you will walk out."

The nurse told me she was of Irish descent, and she was just wonderful putting me at ease, and she answered all my questions. Some may have been silly, but she still answered them to reassure me.

Doctor Clerken popped his head in and said, "How are you, Irish Rose—are you all set?"

I said, "Yes Doctor, and while you are in there, please take a good look and see if anything else needs fixing."

He laughed, and left, saying, "I'll see you shortly."

I walked right to the operating table, and even climbed up on the table myself.

The anesthetist and two other nurses were there helping me.

Doctor Clerken arrived with two assistants and said, "Have a real nice dream, Rose, and we will see you later."

I remember nothing else.

Lily was holding my hand when I came around, and I vaguely remember her saying, "It's all good news."

I remember many nurses, and many people around, and again I heard Lily say, "All went very well, and you are fine."

I tried to answer her, but I just could not get the words out.

"You try to get some rest now as Piers is here to take me home, and I'll see you in the morning," she said.

I must have gone back to sleep because it was next morning when I awoke again. I was still in the recovery room, but a nurse told me that they were transferring me to a ward very shortly.

Doctor Clerken had requested that recovery keep me overnight to keep an eye on me.

He told them I was a special case, so I needed extra care and attention.

I found this out later from one of the nurses.

I had my own private ward, with a big sign on the door that read: "Patient not to have any solids." I had tubes from practically every opening in my body, and very little, or no discomfort at all.

Doctor Clerken and his team arrived, and he checked the wound and told me what they had done during surgery.

They had removed the mass and a small portion of my stomach, but they also removed my gallbladder, as I had polyps and gallstones.

Doctor Clerken said everything was benign, so I should be back better than ever in about six to eight weeks, and no further treatment was required.

I spent seven days in the hospital, and I received so many flowers that I had the nurses spread them around the other wards.

Doctor Clerken came every day with his team, and Lily came and sat with me all day. She watched TV while I dozed off, which was just on and off for short spells.

Brian and his parents came twice, and Piers dropped in each day, when he dropped Lily off.

My colleagues from work kept popping in, so time went quickly.

I was up walking one day after surgery, pulling my tubes along with me.

I had no pain whatsoever, and I did not need pain medication after the second day.

I had the tubes removed the day before I was to go home, but first, I had to eat something, and they had to see if I passed it. Well, I passed it. I guess all my insides were back in place.

Brian and Lily came to bring me home, and I was to return to Doctor Clerken's office in ten days to have my staples removed, all forty-one of them.

I spent the next ten days relaxing and getting stronger. I made several phone calls to everyone I knew, and told them I was all right and thanked them for the flowers and cards and all their support, especially their prayers.

I noticed Brian and Lily were getting along great, and I am sure his mother Kitty was pleased as punch.

Lily did my hair for me the morning I was to go to have my staples taken out in Doctor Clerken's office. I looked pretty good, considering what I had just gone through.

Beth from the office was taking us this morning. All three of us arrived at the doctor's office on time, exactly 11:00 a.m. His nurse came out to take me in, and she removed the staples.

She told me Doctor Clerken had an emergency that morning but his wife, Doctor Amy, would check me out in a few minutes.

I sat about five minutes in his office when in walked this tall blonde woman.

She took my hand, held on to it, and said, "Rose, I am Doctor Amy—how are you doing?"

I felt myself tremble, as she looked so familiar, I think it was the woman in my dreams, but I never saw her face in my dreams. On the other hand, did she remind me of someone I knew?

She sat down beside me and said, "I need to check that wound; no need to get back up on the table. I can see it from here. It's healing beautifully, and you should be back on your feet very shortly."

I saw her check her diary and then she said, "We need to see you again in three weeks, so let's make that appointment before you leave the office.

"My husband said you are Irish," and she looked at me with a smile on her face.

"Yes," I replied. "I was born there, and I only came here on a two-year assignment for my job. I work in the airline industry," I told her.

"I recently went out to Ellis Island on the ferry to see all the immigrants' names," she said.

"Is Rose Kelly a very popular name in Ireland?" She asked.

"Kelly yes, but Rose is not that common, at least I don't know of many," I replied.

"Are you any relation to Grace Kelly? I understand her ancestors came from Ireland." She asked.

"Not that I know of, but I guess we all came from the same clan years ago," I said.

"My brother had an Irish girlfriend once called Rose Kelly. She lived in Dublin, and he met her while on a golfing tour there. He called her his 'perfect Rose.'"

I suddenly felt faint, and she asked if I was feeling okay.

I said, "Was your brother's name Kedrick?"

"Yes! Oh my God—are you Rose?" and she jumped up from her chair, and kept saying, "I can't believe it; here in New York we found you, after all this time."

I said, "What do you mean?"

"We have spent years looking for you, and I even went to Ireland twice, as late as last year to find you. Wait until I telephone him," and she put her arm around me.

I said, "Telephone who?"

"Kedrick, of course," she said.

"But Kedrick was killed in a plane crash," I said, and I was trembling all over.

I felt faint, and she noticed, and she ran and got me a glass of water.

"Oh! Rose, my dear," and she put her arms around me, and she told me the story I so wanted to hear.

WAS IT A DREAM?

She held my hand as she told her story.

"I had dinner with Kedrick and Gary, who was my boyfriend then, after the fundraiser, and we drove him to the airport to catch his plane. We nearly missed it, but they had waited for him. I often wished we had in fact missed it.

"It was a private jet, so they were not tied to a strict timetable.

"Shortly after takeoff, it just fell to the ground and broke up. I understand the engines failed or stalled.

"Kedrick had given all his bags and gear to his caddie, a young man from his golf school, so he was sitting near the rear, all alone, and he was thrown clear of the plane when it broke up, before it burst into flames.

"He was still strapped to his seat when found, but he had serious head injuries, and both legs were broken. He was lucky not to have been burned, like all the others.

"Looking back, I think someone was praying for him, because being in a coma it stopped the brain from swelling, and he has no long-term brain damage.

"Yes, I feel God was watching over him," and she went on to tell me the rest of the story.

"Kedrick was the only survivor, but for two days after the crash, it was thought it was the caddie that survived. It was only when I went to the morgue to identify the body that I realized the mistake. They did look alike, and as you probably know, Kedrick never carried any identification on his person.

"The media had it wrong, and I do not think they ever corrected the story.

"Gary and I took turns sitting with Kedrick, and his friends flew up from Cape Town on the weekends to sit with him. We had a schedule drawn up so that someone he knew was with him at all times, just in case he awoke.

"He has such wonderful and considerate friends; they were always there for him, and me.

"A month after the crash, I had him transferred to the hospital where I worked; the nurses there looked after him as if he was one of their own sons or brothers.

"The doctors assured me that he would eventually come out of the coma, but they had no idea when this would happen. They were also not sure what his mental condition would be, and if his memory would be affected. All we could do was wait, and pray that he would be normal.

"The days became weeks, and no improvement, but we kept our vigil and hoped for the best.

"Barry mentioned you, but we had no idea how to contact you. Kedrick had kept his relationship with you very much under wraps, until his divorce was final.

"All his personal items, his wallet and briefcase with his phone and address book in it, were all burned in the crash. We decided to wait until he came out of the coma and then contact you. To look at Kedrick it seemed as if he was in a deep sleep; some angel somewhere was looking over him.

"Weeks became months, and then one weekend Barry arrived and said, 'Amy, wouldn't the phone company have a record of Kedrick's calls to Rose?'

"'You know, I never thought of that—how can we get them?' I asked him.

"'Well, you had the phone disconnected, but I'm sure there is something we could do,' he thought for a moment and said, 'I know some people in the phone company, let me ask them when I get back to Cape Town.'

"I knew Barry had met you, and he also knew Kedrick cared about you very much, and it worried him that you didn't know what happened."

Did I have Barry all wrong? I asked myself under my breath as she went on to tell me about the day Kedrick eventually woke up.

"Kedrick was in a coma for nearly a year now. Barry had been to visit him and had brought him some roses for his room. The nurse told Barry she thought she saw Kedrick's fingers move during the night, and she watched him for a long time, but nothing else happened. As the shift changed, the relief nurse thought she saw some movement too; this time his eyelids flickered. They called in the head nurse, who in turn called in his doctors. They did see some movement, and ordered that he be monitored on a twenty-four-hour basis.

"Five days later, he opened his eyes. They called me to his bedside, but he was completely disoriented. He kept mumbling something, but we could not tell what he was trying to tell us.

"I called Barry to tell him since he had gone back to Cape Town, and he said he had located your telephone number, but it was disconnected, and there was no forwarding number available."

"Yes, I had moved," I told her.

"Well, Barry flew back up that evening and sat with Kedrick for the next few days; actually we took turns, but he was still very disoriented and rambling on and on. He really didn't know any of us. I was so upset, and there was nothing I could do. I just felt so frustrated. I was his only sister, and I loved him so much.

"I was throwing out the wilted roses and had a good one in my hand when I heard Kedrick say, 'Amy, let me smell that rose.' I nearly let everything drop in the excitement as I turned around to see him looking at me with his hand outstretched.

"He smelled the rose, and then started talking normally, asking many questions like, 'What happened, and where am I?' I just hugged him, sat on his bed, and told him where he was, and why he was there.

"He said he remembered nothing of the crash, and he really did not believe me when I told him he was out for nearly a year. He thought it was just a few days.

"He kept asking if you knew or if I had been able to contact you.

"I told him I would contact you immediately, which was the only thing I could think of at this time. I did not want to upset him by telling him we could not locate you.

"He said, 'She probably thinks I am dead. Amy, you have got to tell her now.'

"As the weeks went by, he made great progress, and now the therapy began to get him back on his feet and walking again. He kept asking if I had contacted you; every time I was with him he asked. I eventually told him how both Barry and I had tried but failed to make contact with you. I told him the story about the phone, and that it had been disconnected. Rose, I think this made him all the more determined to get well, because he looked at me and he seemed to think for a second before he said, 'Well, I'll just have to go find her myself then.' He had no phone in his room; it was not permitted, and this frustrated him somewhat. The doctors thought it was better this way.

"As the months and then years went by, he made better progress than expected. I think it was you and his determination to find you that made it possible.

"He constantly spoke about you, and as soon as he was able to fly, he got the doctor's permission to go find you. He had no photo of you; did he ever have some taken?"

"No, we never got around to doing it," I replied.

"I flew with him to Ireland, and he came back very upset that we didn't locate you, but this made him all the more determined. He kept saying, 'I know she is out there someplace, and I will keep looking until I find her.'

"He moved back to Cape Town and bought a new condo near the water, and that's where he still lives.

"He had no permanent brain damage, and he has completely recovered from all his injuries.

"He told me later that the day he woke up was also your birthday.

"He still finds it hard to believe that a whole year had gone by while he was in his coma, but thankfully, his memory came back; he has had no relapses.

"Last year we went back to Ireland again, this time with Gary. We looked everywhere because he knew you were alive somewhere, but he also knew you thought he had died.

"We even went to the authorities, and all they had was Mary Kelly's with that date of birth, no Rose's, and each one they checked out had moved on.

"He never gave up on finding you. He became more and more obsessed with finding you as the years went by.

"He spent three years in rehab and could not play golf professionally again, but he opened up a golf school, and just last year built an eighteen-hole golf course.

"He went back to Ireland nearly every year since he got out of rehab, but you had moved, and no one seemed to know where to, and he didn't have an address of any of your friends or even know their names. He did not know where your family came from, or where they lived. Ireland is full of Kelly's. He found this out when he went to check the phone directory.

"He came back again last year with my husband and me, but again, we came up blank.

"After the plane crash, I had to close up his condominium in Cape Town. I disconnected his phone, and a year later when he regained conscious-ness, he told me to sell it.

"I kept him with me in Johannesburg. I had married my husband Gary by this time also.

"It was a good five years before he was back to nearly normal and could return to work, not playing just teaching.

"He has a few grey hairs beginning to show around the temples, and when he gets tired, he has a slight limp in his left leg, but we are so pleased he has come through it so well." By this time, she was repeating herself, and she was nearly out of breath.

I was reeling, and my mind was racing a mile a minute. *Is this another one of my dreams?* I kept saying to myself.

"Is he married?" I asked her.

"Oh no! He never gave up hope of finding you.

"He did date off and on, but nothing serious. I think it was more for female companionship, nothing else," she said.

"By the way, did you ever marry?" She asked.

"No. I could never find anyone to match up to Kedrick. He was—*is*—my soul mate," I replied.

She went on to tell me that she would contact him over the weekend, but that he was away on a long business trip this week. "But I expect him back soon. He usually calls to tell me when he is due home, and what flight he is on.

"I expect he will call you as soon as I make contact with him. Do we have your telephone number on file?" she asked.

"Yes, but I will give it to you again, just in case," I said, and I wrote down the number on a piece of paper and handed it to her.

My hands were still trembling, and I was breathing very quickly.

"Let's make that appointment," she said, and we headed to the reception area.

Beth and Lily were there, but I never said anything to them, just yet.

I wanted to surprise Lily, so I told Doctor Amy not to mention it to her or Beth.

I had to pinch myself to make sure it was not another dream. It all had to sink in first.

Lily asked Beth if she would like to come in and have a snack, but she declined, saying, "I have to get back to the office. Thanks anyway."

I told Lily to make a cup of tea. "I have something to tell you, something big—very big," I said.

She was speechless when I told her. She just stared at me with a blank look on her face. Then she started talking in broken sentences. She kept saying, "Are you sure; are you positive?

"Beth was wondering why it took so long in the doctor's office, now we know," she said.

"Dreams do come true, and everything happens for a reason," I told her.

We just hugged each other for several minutes. I was on cloud nine.

Then I began to think, *What do I say to him? Will things be the same as before?*

It has been a long time. Suppose he does not ring, and for the next two days, I could not sleep or eat.

Next week came and went, and no phone calls.

I made up excuse after excuse: he was still away, and Doctor Amy could not contact him.

The second week came and went, and still, no phone call. Still I made up excuse after excuse.

Well, next week I go back to the doctor's office, and I will find out from Doctor Amy what happened.

Maybe he had given up on ever finding me, and had gone on with his life.

Maybe Amy just said he was away on business, just to cover for him.

No, it's nothing like this, I said to myself, there has to be an explanation.

I was able to drive to the doctor's office for my appointment, and Lily came with me.

I really did not know how I felt. I was very confused, frightened, and yet I was excited.

Amy had said he was looking for me, then why hadn't he called? Again, I made up excuses.

I was early for my appointment, and I sat with Lily in the waiting room pretending to look at magazines.

The nurse came out and called my name, and I got up to follow her.

She put me in Doctor Clerken's office; he came in and asked how I was doing, and he checked the wound. He said, "Everything looks good, so I will not need to see you for three months."

He never mentioned anything about Kedrick, and I thought, *That is it; Kedrick has moved on.*

Doctor Clerken picked up my chart and said, "Rose, I need to pop next door to get you some painkillers in case you get spasms; this happens sometimes when the wound is healing. Wait here and I will be right back." He was smiling at me as he said this.

I was looking at the posters, and I had decided to ask him when he came back if Doctor Amy was in, and could I see her.

I heard the door open and a voice say, "Rose, Rose, my perfect Irish Rose." I turned and there was Kedrick.

We just fell into each other's arms, and both of us cried and sobbed loudly for what seemed like an eternity.

Finally, he said, "We have a lot of years to catch up on, but first, when you are well enough to travel, we will go back to our hotel in Paris (that's if it is still there), but we know the Eiffel Tower is still there. I had arranged to meet you there before the plane crash, and I have something to ask you. We can pick up where we left off."

We just held on to each other so tightly, and we both knew we would never be apart again.

"Dreams do come true."

Deep down, I knew that Nana had something to do with this. I just knew.

THE LOST YEARS

Kedrick planned to stay in New York for three weeks. Lily, who by now had accepted the fact that there was a Kedrick, and he really was here, was leaving to go home on the Friday before Kedrick was to leave. He was leaving on Monday.

It was wonderful introducing him to all my friends, including Piers and Brian and all my work colleagues. Kitty and Patrick, Brian's parents, were speechless when they heard the story. First time I saw Kitty at a loss for words.

He spent from early morning until late at night with me at my place, but slept at his sister's at night. I only had two bedrooms, and it would be uncomfortable for me to share mine so soon after major surgery. His suggestion, not mine; I guess Doctor Clerken had told him so.

He filled me in on all that happened to him, and how Amy was unable to contact him until a few days before he flew over to surprise me. He told me he had gone to London on a business trip and had decided at a moment's notice to fly over to Ireland to see if the detective he had spoken to on his previous trips had found out anything about my whereabouts. He said he was sitting in the detective's office at Dublin Castle when in walked another detective from a suburban office, and he joined in the conversation.

"He listened to my story and said he had heard my name somewhere. He thought it was his inspector that had mentioned it. He called the inspector, a Mister Looney, and sure enough, he had known a Rose Kelly. My heart leaped. Could it be the Rose I was looking for? I gave him your description, and he said it sounded very much like you. He said he knew where you lived, and he would try to contact you and call me at my hotel that evening. He would not give me any more information, said he could not. This was the first real lead I had in all the years I was searching for you.

"Inspector Looney called me very late saying he had dropped by your house only to find you had it rented out, and you had gone to work in New York. The tenants had no address for you as all the paperwork was processed through your solicitor.

"They gave me her name, but I could not contact her. Her voicemail said she was out of the office for two weeks.

"I called Amy at once to tell her the news, and of course, you know what happened next. Rose, I was nearly there. I was hot on your trail, but Amy beat me to it."

He went on to tell me that he always knew he would find me someday, but had assumed I thought he was dead, as the media had it wrong and they never corrected the story.

He was afraid I might have gone on with my life as the years passed by, and possibly even gotten married.

"Rose, I would have tried to win you back. If you wanted me to, if that had been the case." He said as he held my hand.

"I had made up my mind never to marry," I told him.

"Never?" he said.

"Yes, I put my career as a top priority after your death, I mean plane crash," I said.

"Well, I have to see if I can change your mind sometime," and he gave me a big kiss.

He was very careful when he hugged me, as I was still tender but not sore from the surgery.

Something was still troubling me, and that was his friend Barry, so I decided to ask him all about what I had seen on the yacht that night so long ago. Even now, after all this time, it still bothered me. I needed answers.

I told him what I had seen, and he laughed and laughed, and finally told me the story.

"Barry is a diamond merchant and carries very valuable merchandise on business trips.

"He has been robbed twice, and the insurance company gave him a real hard time; he actually lost out big time on both occasions.

"Once while traveling with me, he had this idea about the golf balls and said, 'Who would suspect a guy carrying a box of golf balls?'

"He had a couple dozen made up, and now puts his diamonds in two or three to a box of balls, and he has not lost any merchandise since."

I thought it was a brilliant idea too, and it is all above board.

"He has always had all the legal paperwork to export diamonds—legal diamonds.

"Oh Rose, why didn't you mention this to me before—has this been bothering you ever since?" he asked.

"I was going to, in Paris, when we next met there," I said.

"Actually, Barry met a lovely Australian girl, and they got married about six years ago, and they now have three children. He has really settled down, and he does not travel as much nowadays as he loves to spend as much time as possible with his children. He is a changed man, Rose," he said. "I guess this is what he was looking for all his life—family."

He sighed, and again he said, "Family."

"The golf club I have just built is part owned by him. The golf school is all mine, and Barry does not interfere in the running of the golf club at all. He lets me do all the planning.

"We have a great staff, which is how I could just take three weeks off to come here, as I know it is in safe hands. I would have come here anyway, just to be with you again and hold you close.

"I have a lot of hugs and kisses to catch up on." He held me close as he spoke, and we just held hands.

Brian and Lily had really hit it off, and Lily was out every day with Brian when he was off duty, and the other days she just went shopping.

She wanted Kedrick and me to have some space, as we had a lot to catch up on.

Lily loved him from the first day she saw him in the doctor's office, that wonderful day when we found each other again.

It was all arranged that I would fly to Paris for my birthday in October, just over two months away. Kedrick insisted on flying to New York to accompany me. "I don't want you lifting anything," he said.

"I will ring you every day until then, and I will take a few weeks off so that we can spend some time in New York afterwards with my sister and her family."

His sister Amy had two boys, ages five and seven, and he liked spending as much time as possible with them.

We did have dinner with them the week before he was to go back, and I felt so comfortable in their company. Even though they are my doctors, we put the doctor-patient thing aside for now.

I did find out something interesting during the meal.

When I first met Doctor Gary Clerken in his office, he told his wife Amy that he had seen a patient named Rose Kelly, and that she fits the description of Kedrick's friend from Ireland.

He was the one that asked Doctor Amy to see me after the surgery and see if she could check me out, and of course, the rest is history.

Soon it was time for Lily to go home, and Brian was taking her to the airport.

Kedrick and I said our goodbyes to her at my apartment, and he was staying over with me for the weekend. He was leaving on Monday, so we were all alone for a few days.

Lily was a great help to me, and she told me that Brian was coming to Ireland later in the year for some vacation, and he would be staying with her.

I bet Kitty was pleased, or maybe not, if she thought Lily was coaxing him to go live in Ireland. Only time will tell.

The weekend was just like old times. We even heard our song, "Strangers in the Night," on the radio. I told him that this is what had gotten me through the rough times.

"I actually bought the record, and every time I played it, which was quite often, I hoped your telepathy thing would kick in.

"I never gave up hope, Rose. I even left my name and phone number at the hotel you had stayed at in Cape Town hoping that someday you would come back there." He said. I went on to tell him about my many plans to do just that.

We dined out on Saturday night, and just lazed around the apartment catching up on the lost years the rest of the time. Somehow, it did not seem like so many years had passed.

Piers dropped by on Sunday to say goodbye to Kedrick, and much later, I found out that Piers had told Kedrick that if he ever decided to marry, it would have been me, or someone like me, that he would have asked.

He was not able to have children, so he had made up his mind never to marry. "Maybe much later in life, when children are not an issue," he had said.

He told Kedrick that he, Kedrick, was a very lucky man to have found such a wonderful girl, and he wished him the very best for the future, whatever it held.

I was lucky to have found such good friends.

"He is a good man, Rose, and I hope we can continue the friendship," he said.

"Piers will always be a big part of my life; he was there for me when I needed him, and I will be there for him if he ever needs me," and then I told Kedrick all about his illness.

Remember the old saying, "A good friend is like a four-leaf clover: hard to find and lucky to have."

"I'm with you all the way, and if I can help in any way, please let me know, Rose," he said.

All too soon, it was Monday, and Kedrick had arranged to take a taxi to the airport.

He did not want me driving in traffic, just in case I had to brake suddenly and cause some injury to my wound. "I need you in full health in Paris; we have to climb the Eiffel Tower, you know."

He thinks of everything, I thought.

"I'll call you every night," he said, and I replied, "Don't be silly, twice a week will be fine. Or your phone bill will be massive."

"Worth every rand," he said.

We kissed and hugged, and we both knew that soon we would be together again.

I cried all night; I do not know if was with joy or sadness. I guess a mixture of both.

Joy because I had found him again, and sadness that we had missed out on so many years.

It also taught me a lesson to communicate more with people you love. Tell them everything.

Well, now I had something to look forward to.

I returned to work eight weeks after the surgery, and I told them I would be taking three weeks' vacation in October. This had been previously arranged anyway.

That is no problem, I was told. I could take as much time as I wanted, and just go enjoy myself.

I think they were as excited as I was about the whole thing.

Beth said it was like something you would read in a book, or even see in a movie.

Time passed very quickly, and Kedrick did call several times each week.

Somehow, it was as if the lost years were never lost.

My doctor had given me the "all clear" to travel, so I started to pack that suitcase weeks ahead of time. My dresses were left on hangers until the very last minute.

Kedrick arrived on a Friday night, and I met him at JFK.

We were traveling to Paris on a TWA flight on Monday night.

We had dinner on Saturday with Amy and her family, and we just relaxed in each other's arms for the rest of the weekend, sometimes just saying nothing.

Piers said he would drop us off at JFK, and he told us on the way that his treatment was working very well, and he may not have to have one kidney removed.

"I am taking it one day at a time, but I am feeling much better. I want to thank you both for your support," he said.

We checked in at JFK, and soon we were onboard, and on our way.

Kedrick would not tell me where we were staying, so I did not pursue the matter.

We arrived at de Gaulle Airport, and we got a taxi to the hotel.

Yes, it was still there and as beautiful as ever. This time we had the "Royal Suite."

Yes, it had a king bed.

The same waiter was even there; it was as if "time stood still."

We had dinner at the hotel that night, and we planned to go to the Eiffel Tower the next day.

I saw Kedrick talking to the security guard before we went up to the top.

We were all alone up there. I guess it was a Wednesday, midweek, so not too busy.

We just stood there looking out over the city, and then he put his arms around me and said, "Rose Kelly, will you marry me?"

I had expected something like this, but it still came as a big surprise.

After dinner last night, he had given me a beautiful diamond and sapphire necklace for my birthday.

Today was my birthday, the 9th of October. It was also the day Kedrick came back to life again. I remembered that Amy told me this was the day he had come out of his coma.

"Well! Will you?" He asked.

"Yes, yes, of course I will!" and I started to cry.

He pulled a box from his pocket, and he opened it, and handed me the most beautiful ring I had ever seen. It must have been a three- or four-carat diamond, set in platinum, in the shape of a rose. He put it on my finger, and it fit perfectly.

I could not speak; I was still crying.

He just hugged me and said, "I have had that ring for years; I was to give it to you on our last planned trip to Paris, the one that was postponed for several years."

Just then the security guard appeared. He came over and took my hand, saying, "Congratulations, a beautiful ring." His English was quite good.

I found out later that Kedrick had asked him to give us a few minutes privacy, so he had kept the other visitors downstairs for a while.

They all came over to offer their good wishes to us as we left to go down.

We spent three more days in Paris, and I had to pinch myself several times to see if it was another one of my dreams.

When we arrived back in New York, I called my family and all my friends, and Kedrick called Amy, so they all knew.

They all asked the same question: "Have you set a date?"

I had not even thought about it, but I guess we will discuss that before Kedrick goes back.

A NEW BEGINNING

I was exhausted after our Paris trip, and every time I looked at my ring finger and saw this beautiful ring, I had to pinch myself repeatedly, just to make sure it was not another dream.

Kedrick said, "We will take it very easy in New York, only when you feel up to it will we go out. You have to get all your energy back, as we have a lot to look forward to and lots of planning to do."

We still managed to have dinner with all our friends, and with Amy and Doctor Gary—I still call him doctor. We got to Radio City, and took in a Broadway show, and all the usual sights.

One night we sat down to discuss our future. Where will we live? When will we set the date?

We had so many things to think about, and to organize.

Kedrick looked at me and said, "Rose, let's get married as soon as possible, like tomorrow, if that can be arranged."

"We can't do that; we have family to think about," I replied.

"I know, I know. I just can't wait to marry you; I don't want to miss another day without you as my wife," he replied.

I had never asked Kedrick what was his religion.

It did not matter to me, but family may ask the question. I think at this stage of our lives it really would not matter that much to them either.

He surprised me by saying he was Catholic. His first marriage was not in the Catholic Church, so we had no obstacles there.

I thought my parents would be pleased, very pleased.

I told him I would like to finish out my contract with the company in New York; this was up on the 31st of January. "That's only three months away," I said.

I asked him to come to Ireland for Christmas to meet all my family, and we could arrange to get married there.

"How about having a spring wedding?" I looked at him, and he said, "Whatever you want, Rose."

I would resign my job at the end of the contract, and go back home to arrange everything for our wedding.

We discussed where we would live, and Cape Town was the logical solution, as all Kedrick's businesses were located there.

Before he left, it was all arranged, and Amy and her husband were delighted to be getting back to Ireland again.

Kedrick came to Ireland for Christmas, and I was thrilled that my family loved him straight away.

Dad even said, "Now I know why you never gave up hope, or ever found anyone else to match up to him."

We had a wonderful Christmas, and we both flew back the same day, him to Cape Town, and me to New York.

We both knew that it would not be long now before we were together forever and ever.

On the flight back, I decided it was time I went to visit Sally. Mam had said her last letter was not very encouraging. She was crippled with arthritis and was considering going into a nursing home. Betty's death was hard on her too.

"Do call her, Rose; she would love to see you and hear all your good news."

"Yes Mam, I will call her as soon as I get back." I told her.

The following weekend, I called Sally and arranged to fly up there on Friday night, and spend the weekend with her. Her nephew Bill met my flight at Boston Airport, and he drove me to Sally's house. He told me she had finally decided to go to a nursing facility at the end of the month. "It is the best for Sally, and all the family," he said. Sally was so delighted to have me stay. She had a bed made up for me with her mother's best bedspread. She had always lived on her own, ever since her parents had died. This was the original family home, and she had inherited it.

Bill lived just ten minutes away, so he was always there for her. We shared many stories for the next two days, and I told her all about Kedrick, and how I had spent the last twelve years never giving up hope. She gave me her blessing and said, "Rose, I know you will be very happy."

"Did you ever marry, Sally?" I asked her.

She hesitated for a long time and then said, "No, but I am going to tell you a story; it's a story I have never told to anyone before. It was our family secret."

I noticed her eyes were all watery; as she spoke, she was crying.

I put my arms around her and hugged her, but I said nothing. I just waited for her to regain her composure. "Rose, I have always liked you. Imagine, you were just a child when I first met you. You are kind and sincere, so I trust you with the family secret." I hugged her again and I said, "I feel honored you think that way about me."

"Well, where do I start?" she said. "I guess I have to go back to when I was sixteen."

She then started to tell me a story, a story I thought you would only find back in 1950s Ireland. I had heard many stories like it from the nuns over there.

They told me that sometimes girls who got into trouble had their babies at home; the mother then hopped into bed with the baby, and the daughter was sent out to prepare tea for the neighbors. The mother pretended that she was the birth mother to save face with the neighbors.

One thing about the nuns, they never taught us about sex education, never; it was taboo. Looking back, it was awful; we learned from other girls and sometimes by mistake. I was lucky my nana gave me some tips, but then again, even she was reluctant to talk about it.

I never expected to hear it, here in Boston, but I suppose many Irish lived there, and old customs are hard to forget.

THE FAMILY SECRET THAT SALLY HID

The story she told me went as follows. This is my recollection of what she told me about her nightmare.

Sally was just sixteen; she was the youngest of four children: two boys and two girls. Her sister Peggy was eight years older, and she was getting married that summer in Cape Cod. They came from a fishing family, and both boys took after their father and grandfather, all fishermen.

Peggy had all the arrangements made for her wedding to Tom, a local police officer, and Sally was one of her bridesmaids. Their mother was confined to a wheelchair since her stroke, which had happened two months prior. She was getting better with therapy, and it was her dearest wish that she would be able to walk down the aisle with her daughter. Sally was dating a local boy; his name was Liam, and he was also a fisherman. He was just seventeen, and she loved him very much. They planned to marry someday, but their parents said it was just a teenage romance, so they told them to wait a few years to make sure of their feelings for each other. Peggy's wedding was just beautiful, and all the family looked lovely in their finest gear. Her mother was able to walk down the aisle with her, but she had to use a walker to aid her. Peggy's father gave her away, and the bride and groom were going to live just down the road from the family home in Boston.

Peggy had always wanted to marry on Cape Cod. It was the done thing if you wanted to throw a big posh bash.

Sally and Liam crept away from the reception. They had a few beers while sitting on some bales of hay at the back of the hotel. This was Sally's first time to drink, so she felt woozy straight away. They must have fallen asleep because, when they awoke, it was dark. They made their way back to the reception, only to discover that everyone had gone home. Sally could not remember anything after the meal. She did not remember sitting on the hay bales or drinking the beers. Liam left her home; he also told her what had happened on the hay bales. He put her to bed and told her he would see her the next day, after his fishing trip.

Liam never did come back; his trawler was sunk in a freak storm, and all onboard was lost. Sally was devastated, and just took to her room, where she spent most of the next month, just crying her heart out. It was school-break time, so she did not have to go to school. The following month her mother had another stroke, and this time she was paralyzed, from the waist down.

The family decided that it was proper for Sally to stay home and take care of her. It was agreed that Sally would be homeschooled. She had withdrawn from all her friends; it was assumed that it was because of Liam's death, but Sally had another secret: She was pregnant. She could not tell anyone, and she felt she had let everyone down, so she decided to keep it a secret. It was the night of Peggy's wedding that she got pregnant. It was also the first and only time that Liam and she had made love.

Peggy and Tom came over for dinner one Sunday, and Sally prepared a big roast dinner for the whole family. She had become a very good cook; well, she had to cook for the entire family now, especially ever since her mother's second stroke.

It was a real nice family dinner, and at the end of the meal, Peggy said, "Tom and I have some news for you all. We are expecting a baby. I guess I got pregnant on our wedding night," she was giggling as she said this. Everyone was very excited, as this would be the first grandchild. Sally felt sick to her stomach, but somehow managed to act normal during the remainder of the evening.

Sally tried to hide her expanding belly over the next few months. It always made her cry when she saw how proud Peggy was of her belly. One evening, as she got undressed in her bedroom, Peggy popped her head in to say goodnight; she had just dropped by to see her mother, and went upstairs to see Sally.

She just stood there with her mouth wide open, looking at Sally looking at herself in the mirror, her belly in full view. Sally started to cry, and Peggy came and put her arms around her. "Tell me what happened, and who is the father?" she asked. Sally told her the full story. She told her she was so frightened to tell anyone, and Liam was dead, and she did not know what to do. She even thought of suicide, but then she remembered she had her mother to take care of. "Peggy, I am desperate—what am I to do?" she had asked her.

"Just leave it to me and I will tell them downstairs," she said.

"They are going to kill me, Peggy," said Sally.

Peggy went downstairs, and Sally got into bed. She waited for the door to her bedroom to open and for her father to come in to beat her or even kill her. Nothing happened, and she spent the night awake just waiting. Next day her parents told her they would stand by her, but she would have to have the baby adopted. Due to their medical conditions, her mother in a wheelchair and her father a diabetic, she had no choice but to go along with their plans. It was also their plan to keep it a family secret; no one was to know, not even her two brothers.

The midwife, her aunt, took care of Peggy and was also brought into the secret, so both babies were to be born in the family home. Coincidentally, they were both due on the same day; well, they were conceived on the same day.

Soon the day arrived and Peggy went into labor. The midwife was summoned, and twelve hours into Peggy's labor, Sally started hers. The two brothers were sent out to sea, and they were told to stay away for a few days. Both sisters were in full labor, and Sally was having a real rough time. At one stage, it was feared that she would not make it; their mother started praying for both girls. Sally was now thirty-six hours in labor, and her vital signs were not good. The midwife was very experienced, and she decided not to call in a doctor; well, it was still a big family secret. She sedated Sally, and they prayed and hoped for the best. Next morning, when Sally awoke, she was told she had a baby boy, but it had died at birth. Peggy had twins, a boy and a girl. It took Sally several months to get over the birth; she had such a hard labor, and after all that, she had no baby either.

They never showed her his body; they told her they had buried it up at the cemetery in her grandfather's grave. They were still trying to keep the family secret. Betty's twins were christened Bill and Mary. Bill always took very good care of Sally.

I remember when she had finished telling me this story she just looked at me with tears in her eyes and said, "Rose, don't tell the family secret to anyone else."

I told her I would respect her wishes.

"Now you know why I never married. I could never forget Liam." She said as she held my hand. "I also know what you must have gone through."

I still remember her story; she must have gone through hell on earth. I thought about her on my plane trip back to New York.

Sally went into a nursing home later that month, and she died just a few weeks after that. I was not able to attend her funeral, but Bill called me a few days after the funeral, and did he have a story to tell me too. He told me as he was sitting with Sally, when she was near the end, they were discussing some paperwork he had found in his mother's drawer: the family secret—Bill was really Sally's son; he had not died at birth, and Peggy had adopted him as her own.

"She told me she had told you the full story, and I was to ring you and tell you what I had found out. Rose, do you know what she said to me? She just held my hand and said, 'Bill, I always suspected; you had all Liam's mannerisms.' Well, she died later that week and she was so peaceful." He said.

"Bill, I am so glad she knew before she died. I know she is at peace now." I told him I would also keep in touch.

A DREAM FULFILLED

Kedrick was bringing Barry and his family and about twenty friends from Cape Town and England to our wedding. I set about booking a hotel for the reception, and we set the date for April 10th.

My wedding was like a dream, a beautiful story with a very happy ending.

My father gave me away, and all our friends, including Piers and Brian and his family, and all my work colleagues, surrounded us. Beth and her mother came, and they just loved the people there. It was their first time on an airplane, and their first time out of the USA; they were so excited. All my cousins from Chicago, Connecticut, and Boston came, and it was a great family reunion. As I walked down the aisle on my father's arm, I had asked permission to have a beautiful love classic played called "We've Only Just Begun" after the usual "Here Comes the Bride." I had heard this song recently and liked it so much, and Kedrick liked it too, so that is what we had played. It was appropriate as we both felt our life had just begun.

I believe there was not a dry eye in the church. When the priest pronounced us man and wife, Kedrick leaned over and whispered in my ear, "I am now one hundred percent content." I just smiled, but I felt tears welling up in my eyes.

Of course, our first dance had to be "Strangers in the Night"—what else could have been the perfect song for us? Kedrick also asked that "Blue Velvet" be played. He often said my eyes were like blue velvet. We had all the sixties and seventies music played as well, and everyone had a wonderful time. All our guests took the opportunity to spend a little time in Ireland, so they planned a week's vacation after the wedding.

Kedrick and I left for a week in Rome, and then we came back to Dublin, where once again, I packed up my home and put it on the market, and left for Cape Town.

We started to house hunt, and we were staying at Kedrick's condo, the one he just bought two years before.

We found a very large five-bedroom house, with a pool, and all the extras you could think of in a very upscale area, and of course, it was overlooking the ocean, and soon we had it furnished to our taste, what fun that was.

I had some of Nana's things shipped over, things that meant a lot to me. I had some personal items shipped as well, and we settled down to married life and growing old together. We had many years to catch up on.

Nine and a half months later, our daughter, Amy Rose, was born, and twelve months after that, our son, Richard James, was born.

We were so blessed. I thought I was too old to have children, and I also had to consider my recent surgery, but I had no problems at all. I felt that someone was watching over me.

I kept in touch with Piers, and he said he would come to visit us.

Brian got a job in one of the top clinics in Ireland, and he and Lily became engaged.

Their plan was to live in Ireland until Lily got her paperwork sorted out so that she could live and work in the USA. They were then going back to New York and opening up their own practice. I bet his mother Kitty was pleased.

Lily insisted that they get married in Ireland, and not in the USA. There is nothing like a good Irish wedding.

They seemed to be the perfect pair, and if they are as happy as we are, then that is the icing on the cake.

UPDATE

Kedrick and I, together with our children, visit my parents in Ireland once a year, and then go on to New York to visit Amy and her family. Of course, they all come to visit us. When in Ireland, we always drop in to the graveyard to say a prayer for Nana and the rest of the family that rest there. I suspect doctors Amy and Gary and family will return to South Africa someday to open up a practice there.

We have visitors all year long, so I never feel homesick, but how could I; I have my soul mate and my children here.

Brian and Lily are married, and they still live in Ireland. Kitty and Patrick are also moving back to Wicklow.

Pat and her husband, Ted, with their son, Connor, come to visit us as often as possible.

Brenda said she would come soon. She is still trying to make up her mind.

Our friend Piers comes quite often, and his health is good. He did have one kidney removed.

I hear Tim has remarried, and finally settled down. He gave up the music business and now runs a record shop.

Karl did get his fiancée Ria across the wall, strapped her under his car. She was a very brave girl. Love conquers all.

Don was divorced two years after his marriage to Lady Pamela.

Joe, my gardener, and his son, Toby, are doing well, and Joe is engaged to his late wife's sister. This man deserves nothing but happiness. He was my savior.

My neighbor Ellie is still in her assisted-living facility, and when I brought Kedrick to see her, she said, "He is the one worth waiting for." She is now 101 years young I just found out. Before I left, she handed me a little booklet with various sayings. "Something to read on the plane journey back," she said. I put it into my purse and gave her a big hug.

I did read some of the sayings on the journey back, and I found something in Ellie's handwriting just tucked inside the cover. I read it repeatedly, and it stuck in my mind for the entire journey.

I do not know if she wrote it herself or if she had found it somewhere, but I will quote it and hope someone else will find strength and courage from it.

> *If you think—YOU CAN!*
>
> *If you think you are beaten, you are.*
>
> *If you think you dare not, you do not.*
>
> *You have to think high to rise.*

Well, it certainly is something to think about.

I keep in touch with Sally's son Bill and his family. They have promised Mam that they would visit her sometime.

I feel my life is full of love and happiness. I have the best soul mate, friend, lover, and husband in the world, and he is a wonderful father to our children.

Do not ever give up on your dreams.

I will finish with one of Nana's sayings:

> *Having a place to go is Home.*
>
> *Having someone to love is Family.*
>
> *Having both is a Blessing.*

I am blessed, and I am proof that true love always finds a way.